The Case of
the Photo Finish

As more and more athletes climbed up and crowded in, the stands became so full that Nancy began to wonder if there was enough room for everyone.

Cheryl was standing in the top row, right on the end, next to the railing. She was looking out at the crowd, and when she spotted Nancy down below, she waved.

Nancy was raising her hand to wave back when suddenly the cheerful smile left Cheryl's face and was replaced by an expression of surprise and alarm.

In the next instant, Cheryl toppled forward over the railing, flinging out her arms. Nancy watched in horror as Cheryl plunged headfirst toward the pavement below!

Nancy Drew
Mystery Stories

#57 The Triple Hoax
#58 The Flying Saucer Mystery
#59 The Secret in the Old Lace
#60 The Greek Symbol Mystery
#61 The Swami's Ring
#62 The Kachina Doll Mystery
#63 The Twin Dilemma
#64 Captive Witness
#65 Mystery of the Winged Lion
#66 Race Against Time
#67 The Sinister Omen
#68 The Elusive Heiress
#69 Clue in the Ancient Disguise
#70 The Broken Anchor
#71 The Silver Cobweb
#72 The Haunted Carousel
#73 Enemy Match
#74 The Mysterious Image
#75 The Emerald-eyed Cat Mystery
#76 The Eskimo's Secret

#77 The Bluebeard Room
#78 The Phantom of Venice
#79 The Double Horror of Fenley Place
#80 The Case of the Disappearing Diamonds
#81 The Mardi Gras Mystery
#82 The Clue in the Camera
#83 The Case of the Vanishing Veil
#84 The Joker's Revenge
#85 The Secret of Shady Glen
#86 The Mystery of Misty Canyon
#87 The Case of the Rising Stars
#88 The Search for Cindy Austin
#89 The Case of the Disappearing Deejay
#90 The Puzzle at Pineview School
#91 The Girl Who Couldn't Remember
#92 The Ghost of Craven Cove
#93 The Case of the Safecracker's Secret
#94 The Picture-Perfect Mystery
#95 The Silent Suspect
#96 The Case of the Photo Finish

Available from MINSTREL Books

NANCY DREW MYSTERY STORIES®

96

NANCY DREW®

THE CASE OF THE PHOTO FINISH

CAROLYN KEENE

A MINSTREL® BOOK

PUBLISHED BY POCKET BOOKS

New York   London   Toronto   Sydney   Tokyo   Singapore

A MINSTREL PAPERBACK *ORIGINAL*

 A Minstrel Book published by
POCKET BOOKS, a division of Simon & Schuster Inc.
1230 Avenue of the Americas, New York, NY 10020

ISBN: 0-671-69281-X

First Minstrel Books printing August 1990

10 9 8 7 6 5 4 3 2 1

Contents

1 Let the Games Begin   1
2 Warming Up   10
3 A Sticky Clue   20
4 New Information   30
5 Too Many Suspects   40
6 Danger at Dawn   50
7 A Lost Clue   58
8 A Serious Charge   68
9 Lights Out!   78
10 Marta's Confession   88
11 More Dirty Tricks   97
12 A Telltale Photo   107
13 A Secret Source   116
14 Thief in the Night   124
15 Race for the Gold   132
16 Winners and Losers   142

THE CASE OF THE
PHOTO FINISH

1

Let the Games Begin

Nancy Drew pushed her shoulder-length reddish blond hair back from her face and squinted her eyes to get a better look. She leaned to the left, then to the right, trying to see around a tall man in a checked sport coat, but all she could see were the many people who had assembled in front of the River Heights City Hall. The building was draped with colorful flags from around the world, and a big banner over the entrance read, "Welcome International High School Games."

The eighteen-year-old detective and her good friend George Fayne had come for the ceremony being given by the city in honor of the students.

"Can you see? Are the buses coming yet?" Nancy asked.

George, who was a little taller than Nancy, stood on tiptoe and peered over the heads of the crowd. "I don't— Yes, there they are. They're just pulling up to the curb!"

A wave of applause began at the far side of the square, where the bus was, and swept through the crowd toward Nancy and George. When Nancy craned her neck, she could see two lines of young athletes in matching white warm-up suits filing across the open space in front of the City Hall steps. Some of the teenagers looked solemn, almost scared, but others were grinning and waving to the spectators.

"There's Marta," George said.

"The girl who's staying with you?" Nancy asked. Like the Drews, George and her family had volunteered to put up one of the visiting athletes in their home. "Where? Which one?"

George pointed. "The one with the short blond hair, right behind the guy with the headband."

"Oh, yeah, I see her," Nancy said with a nod. "Is she nice?"

"I don't know yet. I've said about five words to her so far, like, 'Hello,' 'Welcome to River Heights,' and 'Your bedroom's this way.'"

"That's more like ten words," Nancy observed with a teasing smile.

George rolled her eyes. "Whatever. No, I guess Marta's all right," she continued. "But her trainer . . . We weren't really figuring on *two* visitors. It's lucky we have twin beds in the guest room. Still, it's a terrific chance to get to know a really great young athlete. I bet we'll be watching some of these kids in the next Olympics." Sports was George's greatest passion, so she was especially excited about the games.

"I like those special passes to the field that host families receive," Nancy added, grinning. "Being able to wander around will be a lot more fun than sitting in the stands the whole time."

Nancy had been looking at the athletes as she and George spoke. "Oh, look," she said, pointing. "There's Cheryl Pierce. She's the one who's going to be staying with us. I hear she's a hot favorite to take home some gold." She sighed, then added, "I wish the company that donated all those warm-up suits had chosen a color other than white. They all look like hospital orderlies."

"Shh! They're starting," George said.

A man in a blue suit had moved over to the microphone at the top of the steps leading to City Hall. As he tapped on the mike, the TV crews turned on their floodlights.

"Ladies and gentlemen," the man began, "I've just received a phone call from the mayor. He asked me to apologize to all of you for being late, most especially to our talented and dedicated young guests from around the world. Unfortunately, his car had a flat tire across town—"

The crowd let out a collective groan, and the TV crews turned off their lights.

"It will be a few more minutes before he can

get here. In the meantime, maybe some of you would like to mingle with our visitors and give them a more informal welcome to River Heights."

Nancy took George's arm. "Come on," she said. "I'll introduce you to Cheryl, and then you can take me to meet Marta. I wonder if they know each other?"

The two friends made their way through the crowd to where the athletes were milling about.

"There she is," Nancy said, then called out, "Cheryl!"

The young woman who looked around was tall and slim, with dark skin and curly long black hair. When she saw Nancy, she flashed a warm smile.

"Cheryl, this is my friend, George Fayne," Nancy said.

"Hi, George," Cheryl said, holding out her hand. "Nice to meet you."

"Hold it!" someone called. "This way!"

Nancy looked around to see a young guy wearing a torn Washington Redskins sweatshirt. He was kneeling on the pavement and aiming a camera at them. A second camera dangled from his shoulder. After snapping a couple of shots, he stood up, grinning.

"That's Eric," Cheryl said. "Eric Land. He's from Washington, too."

"Do you always bring your own photographer to meets?" George asked.

4

"Not really," Cheryl said with a little laugh. "*Athletics Weekly* is putting on a big sports photography contest for high-school students. Eric came up with the idea of following one of the kids who's in the meet. I guess since he's taken some pictures of me before, he thought of me."

"It was nice of you to agree," said Nancy, stepping aside as the photographer leaned past her to get a close-up of Cheryl. "Doesn't he make you a little, um, self-conscious?"

Cheryl laughed again. "I don't even notice him anymore," she said. Then, becoming more serious, she added, "And I figured it would be good publicity for the sport. Track and field events don't really get the attention they deserve."

"And it is so flattering to have your picture always taken as well," a harsh, accented voice broke in. "Easier to be a star before a camera than to win against honest competition."

Cheryl's face froze, and her dark eyes fixed on someone behind Nancy. Looking over her shoulder, Nancy saw an older woman standing there. Her gray hair framed a wrinkled, weathered face, but her body was trim and fit.

"Why, Ms. Roth," George said, stepping forward. "I didn't see you. This is my friend Nancy Drew, and this is—"

"Helga and I know each other," Cheryl said coldly. "I think we met in Italy last time, right?"

"Bologna, in October," the gray-haired woman

5

replied. "Marta was suffering from a bad cough, which allowed you to win the one-hundred-meter sprint."

"I was sick, too," Cheryl retorted. "But I wouldn't have tried to use that as an excuse if I had lost the race. I call that tacky."

"This word I do not know," Helga said. "But you must not expect such good luck this time. Marta is in perfect condition. She will win every event she enters."

"Good for her," Cheryl replied. She turned her back on the trainer. Helga Roth stared at her for a long moment, then walked away.

Nancy took in Cheryl's stony expression, then shot George an inquiring look. She couldn't help wondering if the angry exchange they'd just witnessed was simply because of the competition between the two athletes or if there was something more to it.

"I guess I'd better go," George said apologetically to Nancy and Cheryl, then followed Helga.

"Marta and her trainer are staying with George's family during the meet," Nancy explained.

"I'm sorry if I was rude," said Cheryl. "I don't mind competition. In fact, I need it. Good opponents make for better race times."

"Hey, I like that," Eric said from just behind her. "It'll be a great quote for our article."

"*Your* article, Eric," Cheryl reminded him.

"Please don't get me any more involved than I already am. I have other things to think about—like winning a race—remember?"

Eric merely grinned and snapped another close-up of Cheryl and Nancy.

"I hate people who brag," Cheryl said to Nancy. "It's even worse when they can't live up to their words and then make all kinds of excuses. I mean, for Helga to say I didn't win that race in Italy fair and square . . ."

As she listened to Cheryl, Nancy couldn't help wondering about the competition between Cheryl and Marta. Nancy had earned a reputation as a first-rate amateur sleuth in River Heights, and from what she had just learned, it sounded as though the competition might provide some intrigue as well as plenty of excitement.

"Do you know a lot of the athletes here?" she asked Cheryl.

Cheryl shook her head. "Far from it," she replied. "I've met some of the American kids, of course, and a few of the ones from Europe. I've been to two big meets over there."

"That must have been exciting for you."

"You bet it was." Cheryl's dark brown eyes sparkled. "I never thought I'd get to see Europe before I even got out of high school. You see, my mom works in the post office back in Washington, and we don't have a lot of money for traveling.

But after I started winning at regional track meets, some people in my neighborhood organized a committee and raised the money to send me to these international meets."

"That must make you feel really good," Nancy said warmly.

"Oh, it does," Cheryl agreed. "But it's kind of a burden, too. Everyone has such high hopes for me. I feel like I have to win. And if I don't, if I have an off day—and that can happen to anyone—it's not just me I'm letting down. It's all my supporters, too."

"That's a lot of pressure to be under," Nancy said sympathetically. "I know what it's like when everybody expects you to succeed. It's hard to keep that from getting in the way."

Glancing over Cheryl's shoulder, she noticed a familiar face in the crowd. "Oh," Nancy said, "there's my friend Bess Marvin. Come on over and meet her. I think you'll like each other."

At that moment, however, the man in the blue suit tapped on the microphone again, and Nancy and Cheryl turned to listen.

"Ladies and gentlemen," he began, "I'm happy to say that the mayor is now here with us to welcome our honored guests. Will those of you who will be participating in the River Heights International High School Games please take your places in the stands?"

He motioned toward a set of temporary bleachers made of a pipe frame and wooden planks. Nancy recognized them as the ones that showed up in the River Heights High gym whenever a winning streak drew extra fans to basketball games.

"Excuse me," Cheryl said. "I'd better get over there."

"Sure," Nancy replied. "I'll see you after the ceremony."

Young athletes in their white warm-up suits began heading for the bleachers. Those who got there first had to clamber over the lower benches to reach the upper rows. This slowed them down, and a traffic jam developed at the bottom of the stands.

As more and more athletes climbed up and crowded in, the stands became so full that Nancy began to wonder if there was enough room for everyone. Cheryl was standing in the top row, right on the end, next to the railing. She was looking out at the crowd, and when she spotted Nancy down below, she waved.

Nancy was raising her hand to wave back when suddenly the cheerful smile left Cheryl's face and was replaced by an expression of surprise and alarm.

In the next instant, Cheryl toppled forward over the railing, flinging out her arms. Nancy watched in horror as Cheryl plunged headfirst toward the pavement below!

9

2

Warming Up

Nancy held her breath. Cheryl reached desperately with one hand for the pipe railing. She had almost fallen beyond reach of it, but she managed —just barely—to get a hold on the rail. Then Cheryl's body jerked around and banged into the end of one of the footboards.

But the young athlete didn't lose her grip on the railing and hung suspended ten feet above the ground. Nancy thought she saw Cheryl wince, but the athlete managed to find a foothold on the piping, and she climbed carefully down to the ground. A group of spectators bunched around her.

Nancy dashed through the crowd toward the stands, and as she drew nearer, she heard somebody ask Cheryl if she'd been injured in the accident.

"Accident!" Cheryl exclaimed in a loud voice. "No way! Somebody shoved me. And I bet I know who it was, too!"

Cheryl glared up at the stands, and Nancy followed the direction of her gaze. There, at the railing, looking down, was blond-haired Marta, the runner whose trainer had confronted Cheryl a few minutes earlier.

"Come on, admit it, Marta," Cheryl called up to the stands. "You were right behind me. You saw your chance to make sure that you won an event or two this weekend. So you gave me a little push, right?"

Marta's face turned bright red. "This is a very serious thing you are saying," Nancy heard the girl say in a shaky voice. "I am not at fault if you are clumsy and trip. You must watch your step better."

"You're the one who'd better watch your step," Cheryl retorted. "If I—"

"Ladies and gentlemen," the voice over the loudspeaker boomed. "His Honor, the mayor."

Apparently, no one had noticed the disturbance except for a small circle of people at the end of the stands where Cheryl had fallen. Cheryl gave a frustrated shrug and turned away from her argument with Marta.

The mayor, a tall man with wavy gray hair and bushy eyebrows, stepped up to the microphone and raised his arms to acknowledge the applause.

11

As the clapping died away, he began: "My friends, our city of River Heights is honored to welcome some of the finest, most dedicated young athletes in the world. This weekend, the eyes of sports fans everywhere are turned toward River Heights."

Nancy tuned out. Whatever the mayor had to say, it could hardly be as important as the question she had to grapple with. Had someone just tried to push Cheryl off the stands? Ten feet wasn't an enormous drop, especially for an athlete, but Cheryl could easily have pulled or bruised a muscle. Even a minor injury could hinder her performance in the meet. Would Marta do such a thing?

Nancy glanced up into the stands again. Marta's trainer, Helga, was sitting next to Marta, looking even grimmer than before. Was she concerned because of the attack on Cheryl and the accusation against Marta? Nancy wondered. Or because the attack had failed?

Struck by a sudden idea, Nancy glanced around at the crowd until she spotted Eric's Redskins sweatshirt a dozen feet away. She started edging toward him.

"Eric?" she said in a low voice, so as not to disturb the mayor's speech.

"Oh, hi," he said, startled.

Several spectators looked around, frowned, and said, "Shh!"

Nancy leaned closer to him and whispered, "Did you see what happened before, when Cheryl fell from the stand?"

"I sure did," he muttered. "That was a close call. I hope it doesn't hurt her chances in the meet."

"Did you get any pictures of the fall?"

"Well . . . I can't be sure. I glanced over just as she started to fall. It took me a moment to get the camera up to my eye, so I missed the first few seconds of the action."

"Oh," Nancy said, disappointed.

"I managed to grab a few shots, though," Eric continued.

"Would your photos show who was standing near her when she fell?" Nancy asked.

"Maybe. It depends on the field of view. I zoomed in pretty quickly. Why?"

"Cheryl said that somebody pushed her," Nancy told him. "I'd like to know if she's right. Because if she is, whoever did it might try again."

Eric raised his eyebrows, and a look of excitement came into his eyes. "Wow, what a story! 'Danger Stalks Teen Track Star.' Or better yet, 'Prize Photos Hold Crucial Clue.'"

"Listen, this isn't a game," Nancy cautioned him. "Cheryl might have been hurt just now. Her fall could have been an accident, of course. But if it wasn't, and if your pictures can help head off another attack—"

13

Eric looked apologetic, and his cheeks flushed. "I know, I'm sorry," he said. "I can't help talking like that sometimes. I really do want to help. The only thing is, the camera's loaded with color slide film. It might be hard to find a lab that'll develop it in a rush."

"See what you can do, okay?" Nancy said. "And if I can help—"

A burst of applause signaled the end of the mayor's speech. Nancy looked up to see him come down the steps and start shaking hands with the athletes and the other guests as they filed out of the bleachers.

"Excuse me," Eric said. "I need a shot of Cheryl with the mayor." He hurried away, already raising one of his cameras to his eye. Nancy looked after him and shook her head. Obviously, Eric was totally wrapped up in his project. She just hoped he remembered to take a break from taking pictures long enough to get his film developed.

"Ground Control to Nancy Drew," a voice said. "Come in, please."

Nancy glanced around and saw Bess Marvin, George's cousin. "Oh, hi, Bess," Nancy said. "I noticed you in the crowd just before the mayor's speech, but there wasn't time to say hello."

Bess's blond hair shone in the sunlight. Focusing her sparkling blue eyes on Nancy, she said,

14

"You look very thoughtful. The mayor's speech must have made quite an impression on you."

"I didn't hear a word of it," Nancy replied. She quickly filled Bess in on Cheryl's fall.

"Hey, I saw that! She's your guest?" Bess paused and studied Nancy's face for a moment. Then, rolling her eyes, she said, "Uh-oh. I know the signs. You smell a mystery. You think her fall wasn't an accident, and you're planning to find out who pushed her. Right?"

"Right," said Nancy. "I'm not sure of what really happened. I suppose it's possible that it was an accident, but Cheryl accused another runner named Marta, who's staying at George's house. Marta denied it, of course."

"Marta—she has short blond hair, right?" Bess asked. "I met her. What's the problem?"

Nancy frowned. "I don't know either of them, so I don't have any reason to believe one more than the other. I'll just have to keep my eyes open."

Bess shook her head. "I guess I'm lucky. The girl who's staying at our house is a fifteen-year-old named Marie-Laure, from the South of France. She's really shy and doesn't know a word of English, but she's got the longest legs I've ever seen. She does the high jump."

Nancy noticed Cheryl walking in their direction with a girl with a brown ponytail and a tall

15

blond guy whose deeply tanned face ended in a pointy chin. Their warm-up suits showed that they, too, were participants in the track meet.

As the trio came up to Nancy and Bess, Nancy said, "Cheryl, are you okay? That looked like a nasty fall, even though you did a great job of recovering yourself."

Cheryl rubbed her shoulder. "I think I'll have a couple of bruises, but nothing that will stop me from competing. The nerve!" she exclaimed. "Having somebody bad-mouth me is one thing—I can let that just roll off—but when people start shoving me off a grandstand, I draw the line!"

"Are you positive—" Nancy began.

"You bet I am!" Cheryl broke in. "You can ask Annelise. She was right there the whole time." She gestured to the girl and boy she'd been walking with. "Nancy, meet Annelise and Willy. They're from Switzerland, and they both speak better English than I do. The Swiss are incredible linguists, you know."

Willy smiled. "We have to be," he said with only a trace of an accent. "Our country has four official languages—German, French, Italian, and a language called Romansh that nobody outside of Switzerland even knows about. English is the unofficial fifth."

"Five languages," Bess said, shaking her blond

16

head in amazement. "And I thought learning just one extra was hard enough!"

Nancy introduced Bess, then turned to Annelise. "Cheryl says that you saw someone try to push her from the grandstand. Is that right?"

The Swiss girl thought for a moment. "I did not really see what happened," she said. "It is possible that someone bumped into Cheryl, but I did not see it. I'm sorry."

"I think maybe I know what happened," Willy said to Cheryl. "In the crowding, someone pushed into you by accident. Then, when you fell, the person was too frightened to admit what had happened."

"It could have happened like that," Cheryl admitted reluctantly. "But I was sure I felt a hand on my back, shoving me. And Marta was right there. Still, maybe I shouldn't have accused her —not without proof. But I was really furious."

Marta did seem like the most likely suspect, thought Nancy. But she knew it was dangerous to jump to conclusions without evidence. "Is there anyone else who would have reason to push you?" she asked Cheryl.

"No one that I can think of," the runner replied.

Nancy looked around. The crowd had thinned out now that the ceremony was over. George was still there, standing on the steps of City Hall with

Helga, Marta's trainer. They didn't seem to be talking to each other, Nancy noticed. Marta joined them a moment later; she had a knapsack on her back.

Turning back to Cheryl, Nancy asked, "What happens now?"

"Those who wish to go back to the athletic field may take the buses," Willy replied. "Most of us will go to the homes of our hosts."

"Oh, Cheryl, I've got my car here," Nancy said, smiling at her guest. "Would you like a lift back to the house? You could unpack or whatever."

"Sure, that'd be great," Cheryl replied. "Hang on, I have to get my gym bag from the bus."

As she hurried away, Nancy realized that she hadn't seen Eric and his cameras for five or ten minutes. She hoped he'd gone in search of a lab to develop those slides for her.

"It is a pleasure to meet you, Nancy," said Willy, holding out his hand.

"A great pleasure," Annelise echoed, offering her hand as well.

"Thank you." Nancy shook their hands. "It's been great meeting both of you. And good luck in the games."

Cheryl came back as Annelise and Willy were walking away. "They're nice," she observed. "A little formal, but that's just their style. Underneath it, they're really sweet."

The two girls headed for Nancy's car and drove to the Drews' house. Nancy went to the kitchen to fix a snack while Cheryl went up to the guest room to relax for a while. Nancy had finished peeling and slicing some carrots and was starting to prepare a yogurt dip when she heard Cheryl cry out, "That does it! When I get my hands on that little creep, I'm going to tear her up and throw away the pieces!"

3

A Sticky Clue

Nancy dashed out of the kitchen and up the stairs to the guest room, stopping in the open doorway.

Cheryl was standing in the middle of the room, staring down into her open gym bag, which lay on the bed. Her fists were clenched, and she was breathing heavily.

"What is it?" Nancy asked. She could guess who the "little creep" was, but she had no idea what had happened to make Cheryl so angry. "What's wrong?"

"Take a look," Cheryl said angrily, pointing to the gym bag.

Nancy crossed the room to the bed. At first she didn't see anything out of the ordinary in the bag—just shorts, tops, a pair of running shoes, a magazine, and a small bag that seemed to contain toiletries. But everything seemed to have the same yellowish brown tinge.

Then, Nancy noticed a small jar that had rolled into the corner of the bag. The top was off. Reaching in, she pulled the jar out, holding it carefully by the rim.

The label of the jar had the word *Honig* in gold letters across the top and a picture of a bee wearing a golden crown in the center. Nancy didn't need to read the English translation at the bottom of the label. Her fingertips and nose had already told her that the jar had once contained honey—and that the contents were now all over Cheryl's running gear.

"What a mess," Nancy said, frowning. "How did it happen?"

"Somebody put that gunk in my bag, that's how," Cheryl replied. "And I know who! Just wait till I catch up to her!"

"Catch up to whom?" Nancy asked, although she was pretty sure she knew whom Cheryl was referring to.

"Marta, that's who! Or maybe it was Helga, her trainer. It doesn't matter." Cheryl reached into the bag and pulled out what looked like a leather insole. "My orthotics are probably ruined!" she wailed. "Do you know how long it takes to have these things made and fit? And how much they cost? What'll I do?"

"We can try to clean them off," Nancy suggested. "And we can throw the clothes in the washer. They'll be ready in an hour."

Continuing to hold the honey jar by its rim, Nancy held it up to the light. "Did you touch this?" she asked.

"I don't think so," Cheryl said. "But I might have. I reached into the bag to pull out some things, then I felt that guck. Why?"

"There might be fingerprints," Nancy said. "There are a few smudges, anyway. I'll keep the jar safe and take a closer look later. When was the last time you knew for sure the bag was all right?"

Cheryl gave her a curious glance. "You sound just like a detective," she said.

Nancy let out a little laugh. "Well, to tell the truth, I am. I'll tell you all about it sometime. But for now, what about the bag?"

"Let me think." Cheryl knitted her brow in concentration. "Oh, okay—I was looking at a magazine on the bus. When we got to the ceremony, I stuck it inside my bag."

"Would you have seen the honey jar if it was already there?" asked Nancy.

"Well, sure! I remember now, I rummaged around inside for my comb. There wasn't any jar of honey in my bag then."

"And then you left the bag on the bus?"

"Uh-huh. On the luggage rack."

Nancy glanced down. The ID tag attached to the strap of the bag was easy to spot. Anyone could have known the bag was Cheryl's.

"Why do you think that Marta or her trainer put the honey in your bag?" Nancy continued. "Did you see either of them acting suspiciously?"

"Nooo," Cheryl said slowly. "But Marta always takes some special kind of honey wherever she goes. It's part of her training diet."

"*This* kind of honey?" asked Nancy.

"I don't know," Cheryl admitted. "But who else would pull such a dirty trick on me? You heard the way that Helga talked to me. And it *is* German honey, isn't it?"

"But they're not the only Germans at the games, are they?"

"I guess not," Cheryl admitted. "But they're the only ones *I* know. And I know I'm Marta's toughest rival. When we compete together, one or the other of us almost always wins."

The telephone rang, and a moment later, Hannah Gruen, the Drews' housekeeper, called up to Nancy. Hannah had worked for the Drews since the death of Nancy's mother, when Nancy was just three. She was almost a member of the family.

"The phone's for you," Hannah said. "It's George, and she sounds upset."

"Excuse me a moment," Nancy said. "Why

23

don't you take all your things down to the kitchen so we can start cleaning them up."

Nancy went downstairs and took the call in her father's study. Hannah was right. George *was* upset. "Can you come right over?" she asked. "I've got an international incident brewing over here. Helga is accusing Cheryl of theft, and she's threatening to call the police."

" 'Theft'?" Nancy repeated. "What kind of theft?"

"I don't know," George replied. "Every time I ask her a question, she makes another long speech in German. But she's plenty mad, I can tell you that."

Nancy lowered her voice and said, "I've got a problem here, too. But I think it's under control for the moment. I'll be right over."

She hung up and went to the kitchen, where Cheryl and Hannah were looking at the honey-coated clothes and discussing the best way to clean them. Nancy didn't want to alarm Cheryl with Helga's accusation until she knew more about it, so she simply announced that she had to go out for a few minutes.

Cheryl, who seemed preoccupied with cleaning her gear, just said, "Okay. I'll see you later."

Nancy hopped into her Mustang, but a few minutes later she regretted her decision to drive the short distance to the Fayne house instead of walking. She got stuck behind a sanitation truck that was creeping along its rounds, and it took forever before the truck finally pulled over far enough for her to pass. One of the sanitation men waved as she went by, and she gave him a tap of the horn in reply.

George was waiting for Nancy on her front steps. "Hosting an athlete isn't turning out to be as much fun as I was expecting," George remarked with a wry smile.

"Is Helga still mad?" Nancy asked.

George rolled her eyes. "Wait'll you hear!"

Nancy followed George into the house. The German trainer was standing in the middle of the living room with a stormy look on her face. Marta was sitting on the couch, looking scared.

Helga took one look at Nancy and said, "You are not the police."

"No, I'm not," Nancy agreed, keeping her voice friendly. "But I've worked closely with the police many times. Won't you tell me what the problem is?"

"You are a friend of Cheryl Pierce, no?"

Nancy shook her head. "Not really. Cheryl is staying at my house, just as you and Marta are staying at George's. I met Cheryl this morning for the first time. Why?"

"I wish to accuse her of theft and attempted sabotage," Helga replied.

"Those are serious charges," Nancy said. "What was stolen? And what kind of sabotage?"

"Cheryl Pierce is trying to destroy Marta's training regime by taking a most important item from her diet."

"From her diet?" Nancy repeated, looking at the older woman with new interest. "This item that was stolen—it wouldn't be a jar of honey, would it?" She recalled the jar label. *"Honig?"*

Helga stared at her. "How are you knowing this?" she asked. "It was not just any honey, but honey with a special food from the queen bee. Very rare, and very expensive."

"She must be talking about what they call royal jelly," George said to Nancy. "I've seen articles about it."

"So have I," Nancy said. "Ms. Roth, do you have any idea when and where this special honey was taken?"

"It was in Marta's bag—this morning. Now it is gone. Cheryl Pierce must have taken it while the bag was in the bus."

Nancy frowned. First Cheryl's bag had been tampered with, and now Marta's.

"How could Cheryl have known the honey was there?" Nancy asked.

"Everyone on the bus knew. A person made a joke because Marta takes a spoonful with each meal," Helga explained in a serious voice. "It is not civilized to joke about a training regime like that. To try to ruin one is a crime."

From the couch, Marta suddenly said, "This is very upsetting. I depend upon my diet. How will I run my best now?" She looked as if she were about to cry.

George went over to Marta and patted her shoulder. "Hey, no problem," she said cheerfully. "There's a health food store a few blocks from here. I'm pretty sure I've seen honey with royal jelly there. Who knows? It might even be your brand."

"Is this so?" Helga asked. She pulled a map of River Heights out of the pocket of her warm-up suit. "Will you please show me where? I will go at once." A few moments later, she was on her way out the door.

"You must not mind Helga," Marta said after her trainer had left. "She would do anything to help me become champion."

"We noticed," replied George with a laugh.

Nancy looked closely at the German girl, then exchanged a significant look with George. She knew George was wondering the same thing she was: Did "anything" include sabotaging Cheryl? Still, that didn't explain why Marta's things had also been tampered with.

Nancy was mulling over this when the Faynes' doorbell rang.

"Helga must have forgotten something," George said, leaving the room. She returned with a young woman who was carrying a briefcase.

"This is Barbara Williams," George said. "She's a reporter from *United Sports News.*"

"Really?" said Nancy, regarding the young woman curiously. Although she was dressed in a suit, she didn't look old enough to be out of high school yet.

A blush rose to Barbara Williams's cheeks. "I'm not exactly—" she began. "I mean, I'm really freelance. But *USN* said they were very interested in my project. I'm interviewing a lot of the athletes who've come to River Heights to take part in the high school games. Are you"—she pulled a list from her pocket and glanced at it—"Marta Schmidt?"

"I am Marta Schmidt," Marta replied, standing up. "But I am not permitted to give interviews without my trainer present. I am sorry."

"Oh, that's all right," the reporter said quickly. "I understand. Different countries, different customs, right? When will your trainer be available?"

"She left for only a little while," said Marta. "If you can come back in half an hour—"

The telephone rang before the reporter could reply. George answered it, pressed a button to put the call on hold, then beckoned to Marta. "It's for you," she said.

28

Looking surprised, Marta took the receiver. George pushed the button a second time to release the hold, but her finger accidentally pressed the speaker button at the same time.

"Marta Schmidt," a thickly accented voice said from the phone's built-in speaker.

George reached to turn off the speaker, but Nancy grabbed her arm.

"This is a warning, Marta Schmidt. Pay close attention." The voice was drowned out for a few seconds by a loud grinding, scraping noise. Then it continued. "You will quit the games and go back to Germany. If you do not, the results will be very bad for you. This will be your only warning. Quit the games . . . or else!"

4

New Information

The menacing voice fell silent. There was a click, then the sound of a dial tone.

For a moment, Marta continued to hold the receiver so tightly that her knuckles were white. Finally she replaced the receiver in its cradle, but the look of fear on her face remained.

Barbara Williams broke the tense silence. "Wow!" she exclaimed. "Was that supposed to be some kind of joke?"

"If it was, it's not a very funny one," George commented.

"This is horrible," Marta said in a tight voice. "Who is this person to tell me to quit the games and go home? He has no right!"

"He?" asked Nancy. "Or she? What did the rest of you think? Could that have been a woman's voice as well as a man's?"

"It sounded like a man to me," Barbara replied.

"I'm not so sure," George said. "I guess it could have been a woman. What kind of accent was that? German?"

"I think not," Marta said. "It is not easy to tell in a foreign language, but I think that person was not German."

"Wait a minute," Nancy said. "That noise in the middle of the call, remember? It sounded like some kind of machinery, and there was a sort of scraping sound. What could it have been?"

Suddenly Nancy snapped her fingers. "Of course!" she exclaimed. "I've got it."

She started for the door, and George called after her, "Where are you going, Nancy?"

Nancy looked over her shoulder and gave her friend a mysterious smile. "To catch up to some garbage," she replied.

As she pulled her Mustang out of the Faynes' driveway, Nancy saw Helga walking down the block. In her hand she was carrying a small paper bag.

Hmm, Nancy thought, peering at the older woman. She had obviously found the health food store. Had she also had time to find a telephone and make the threatening call to Marta? It seemed unlikely that Helga would do anything to upset Marta during a competition, however—

unless she wanted to divert suspicion from herself and her prize pupil.

After circling the neighborhood twice, Nancy finally spotted the sanitation truck coming toward her. She passed it and continued down the block. Just as she had hoped, there was a pay phone on the next corner. Making a quick U-turn, Nancy caught up to the truck and pulled over to the curb.

"Hi," she said as she walked over to the guy who had waved to her earlier. "I was wondering, did you happen to notice anyone making a call from the pay phone back on the corner, about five minutes ago?"

"Hey," the man said with a smile, "I know you. You're Nancy Drew, right? I saw your picture in the paper a while back. You out detecting again?"

Nancy smiled back. "Something like that," she replied.

"Way to go! Now, let me think." He rubbed his chin and stared up into space for a moment. "Pay phone on the corner . . . Yeah, there *was* somebody there. I remember because I noticed whoever it was was wearing an all-white jogging suit. Not what you'd call super-practical, huh?"

Nancy nodded. "Did you notice anything else about the caller?"

He shook his head. "Nothing."

"Was the person male, female, young, old, short, tall? What color hair?"

"Sorry. All I really saw was a couple of legs and elbows. The rest was hidden behind the phone. I wasn't really paying attention, anyway. You understand, I was busy doing my job." He shrugged. "Look, I'm sorry, but we still have half the run to do. I've got to go."

"Sure. Thanks for your help," Nancy said.

As the truck started moving, the man called out, "Good luck with your case!"

Before driving off, Nancy thought over this latest development in the case. The white warm-up suit made it a safe bet that Marta's threatening caller was involved with the high school games, either as a competitor, an official, or a trainer.

She started her car and drove back to George's house. Barbara Williams was coming down the walk as she pulled up, and the young reporter looked depressed.

"You didn't get your interview?" Nancy guessed.

"Nope," the reporter replied. "I tried every argument I could think of, but Marta's trainer flatly refused. She wouldn't let Marta say a single word. Just claimed she was tired and sent her to bed for a nap." Barbara shrugged. "Oh, well, on to the next interview."

She pulled a sheet of paper from her briefcase and consulted it, then looked around. "Whitworth Drive. Have you ever heard of it?"

"I think it's in that new development near the country club," Nancy replied. She looked curiously at the sheet of paper. "What is that? May I see?"

"It's just a list of the athletes and their hosts. It was in my press kit. I think all the athletes got one, too."

Barbara held it out to her, and Nancy quickly glanced at it before handing the list back. "I see. I was wondering how you knew where to find Marta." And how Marta's mysterious caller got George's phone number, she added to herself. The list was further proof that the caller was someone connected to the games.

"Well, I'd better get going," Barbara said. "By the way, I didn't catch your name."

"I'm Nancy Drew."

Barbara's eyes widened. "The detective? I should have guessed! Say, are you planning to track down the person who threatened Marta Schmidt?"

"I'm going to try," Nancy admitted.

"What a dynamite story! Will you let me in on what you find out? 'Terror Stalks High School Games'—I can see the headlines now!"

Nancy grimaced. She wasn't sure she wanted the case getting a lot of publicity. It would only alarm the contestants and make everyone edgy, and that might interfere with her investigation.

"Maybe later," Nancy hedged, "but for now I'd like to keep this quiet."

As she drove home, Nancy drummed her fingers on the rim of the steering wheel, going over in her mind everything that had happened that day: Cheryl's "accident," the spilled jar of honey that turned out to be stolen from Marta, and now the menacing call to Marta. Each girl seemed convinced that the other was out to ruin her chances in the meet. And maybe that was exactly what was happening, but somehow Nancy didn't think so. The question was, who else would want to hurt them?

Nancy turned into her driveway just as two people in white warm-up suits came down the porch steps. One was the Swiss girl, Annelise. The other was a tall barrel-chested guy with bushy red hair, broad shoulders, and muscular arms. Nancy waved as she brought her car to a halt.

"Hello," Annelise said as Nancy got out of the car. "We walked over to see Cheryl, but she is not in the house now. Oh—this is Ramsay Roberts. He's from Canada."

"Hi, Ramsay," said Nancy. "Are you a runner, too?"

He grinned. "With my build?" he said. "Not a chance! My events are the shot put and the discus throw. Are you into track and field?"

"I'm afraid my event is spectating," Nancy said with a laugh. Turning back to Annelise, she asked, "Did Hannah say where Cheryl went?"

Annelise shrugged. "She went for a run, it seems. I wish she had called me. I would have gone with her. There is nothing like a run to relax the nerves."

Nancy wondered briefly whether Cheryl's run might have taken her past that pay phone on Winding Way. After all, the threatening caller's thick accent might have been a way to hide the *lack* of an accent.

Up the block, a figure in white came loping around the corner. "There's Cheryl now," said Nancy.

"Hi," Cheryl called, coming to a stop in front of them and pulling off her terry-cloth headband. Nancy noticed that she looked uncomfortable when she saw Ramsay.

"What brings you guys this way?" Cheryl asked.

"I was taking a walk and I ran into Annelise," Ramsay explained. "She said she was coming to see you, so I decided to come along. I tried to catch you at the ceremony, but you got away from me." He paused, then added pointedly, "That's getting to be a habit, isn't it?"

"Runners are like that," Cheryl said. "You let them out of your sight for a minute and they're gone."

"Yeah, I noticed," the Canadian replied in a voice tinged with bitterness.

Nancy looked from Cheryl to Ramsay. The tension crackled between the two athletes. There must be some reason Ramsay is so bitter, Nancy thought. And she intended to find out what it was. "Why don't you all come into the house?" she suggested. "I bet I could dig up some cookies and a pitcher of lemonade."

"Thank you," said Annelise. "That would be very welcome. I did not think it would be so warm at this time of year."

In the kitchen, Hannah was just taking Cheryl's super-light nylon shorts out of the dryer. She held them up, looked them over, and said, "There, now, what did I say? They're as good as new. Oh, and I put your shoe inserts on the back porch to dry. I'm sure they'll be fine by tomorrow."

"Doing your laundry?" asked Ramsay. His smile had a mocking edge to it.

Cheryl explained about the overturned jar of honey in her gym bag. "And I know who did it," she concluded, "because we all know she never goes anywhere without her special honey."

"Marta claims that someone stole it from her gym bag," Nancy told Cheryl. "She blames you for the theft."

"That's ridiculous," Cheryl said. "Why would I steal her honey?"

"Why would she pour it on your gear?" Ramsay countered.

Cheryl scowled. "I don't know, but I bet Nancy will find out. She's a famous detective, you know."

There was a short silence, during which Ramsay and Cheryl merely glared at each other. Then Annelise asked, "You are? Really? I have always wanted to see a detective at work. Is it possible I may help you with your case?"

Nancy raised an eyebrow. "Won't the games keep you pretty busy?"

"This is true. But when I am not practicing, I can assist you."

Nancy thought quickly. The person—or people—who was harassing Cheryl and Marta was almost certainly connected to the games. A source of inside information would be very useful, maybe even essential.

"Thanks, Annelise," she said. "I haven't planned my strategy yet, but as soon as I know what it is, I'll ask for your help. Now, how about that lemonade I promised you?"

Nancy took the cold pitcher from the refrigerator, while Hannah put glasses and a plate of freshly baked peanut-butter cookies on a tray. "What do you say to the backyard?" Nancy said to the others. "It's nice and shady."

"Good idea," said Ramsay. He reached for the tray. "Here, let me take that."

Nancy opened the back door and held it for Cheryl, Annelise, and Ramsay, then followed them onto the back porch.

Suddenly Nancy saw a glint of light to her left, behind the bushes at the edge of the yard.

It looked like the reflection of sunlight off a gun barrel—and it was pointing straight at them!

5

Too Many Suspects

"Get down!" Nancy dived forward, catching Cheryl and Annelise in her outstretched arms and pushed them to the floor of the porch.

Behind her, Nancy heard a crash and the sound of shattering glass. Something cold splashed her leg and soaked into her sock.

Ignoring Cheryl's and Annelise's cries, Nancy called out, "You in the bushes! Come out right now, unarmed, or I'll call the police!"

"No, please, don't do that," a familiar-sounding voice called out. "It's just me!"

Nancy got to her knees and peered over the porch railing. Eric Land was ducking through the bushes, protecting his camera and long telephoto lens with his left arm. That was what she had thought was a gun barrel, Nancy realized. The crash had been the pitcher of lemonade breaking.

Eric got clear of the bushes and straightened up. "I'm sorry," he called. "I didn't mean to scare you."

"Well, you *did* scare us," Cheryl said, getting to her feet. She sounded furious. "What on earth did you think you were doing, hiding out there?"

"I wanted to get a few candid shots," Eric explained sheepishly. "You know, 'Track Star and Friends Share Lemonade and Cookies in Host's Backyard.'"

"No lemonade," Ramsay announced, pointing to the broken pitcher. He stood and dusted off his knees. "Not anymore. And the cookies aren't in such great shape either, thanks to you." He started picking up the pieces of broken glass and putting them on the tray.

"Hey, I said I was sorry, didn't I? Here, let me help."

At the back door Hannah appeared, a concerned look on her face. When she saw the broken pitcher, she went and got a broom and dustpan.

Taking them from her, Cheryl said to Eric, "You've done enough already. And let me tell you—the next time you pull a stunt like this, I'm dropping the project and writing to the people at *Athletics Weekly* to let them know how you've been acting."

Eric's face took on a stony look. Turning away from Cheryl, he bent down to help clear up the rubble.

"I'll make more lemonade," Hannah offered. She took the tray of broken glass from Ramsay and started to go inside. "It'll be ready in a jif."

"Thanks, Hannah," Nancy said. She turned back to the others. "Well, let's go sit down. Eric, will you join us?"

"He already did," Cheryl muttered.

Eric gave Cheryl a pleading glance, then looked at Nancy. "Thanks," he replied. "Oh— you know those slides you asked me about? The ones at the ceremony today? I was right. There's no place in town that has the equipment to process them overnight."

"What slides are you talking about?" asked Cheryl. "Of me?"

"I was taking pictures when you fell off the stand," Eric explained. "Nancy thought they might show something interesting."

"Like Marta or Helga shoving me, you mean?"

"I'm not saying it's likely," Nancy cautioned, "but I thought it was worth a try. Eric, is there any way you could send them off for rush processing?"

He hesitated. "I don't think so," he said unhappily. "The thing is, I was shooting so much that I didn't have time to number my rolls of film. I'm not even sure which one it is."

42

"Send them all," suggested Ramsay.

Eric shook his head. "I can't afford to do that. With a rush job, the lab isn't always so careful. If something went wrong, my whole project could be blown. Sorry."

Nancy shot a curious look at him. To most photographers, numbering their film was automatic—practically second nature. It seemed odd that Eric would have forgotten.

"Never mind," Nancy said quickly. "It was just an idea. Oh, good. Here comes Hannah with another pitcher of lemonade. Let's see if we can get it on the table in one piece this time."

Fifteen minutes later, Annelise stood up. "I must go," she announced. "Nancy, thank you for your hospitality. Do not forget that I want to help you detect. Will you be at the country club tonight?"

Nancy blinked. She had forgotten that the River Heights Chamber of Commerce was giving a reception that evening for the athletes and their local hosts.

"Sure, I'll be there," she replied.

Annelise smiled. "Very good. Perhaps we can search for some clues, yes?"

"I hope so," Nancy said. She had been thinking the same thing. The reception would be the perfect opportunity to see all the athletes together. She just hoped there weren't going to be any unpleasant surprises.

Ramsay rose to his feet as well. He thanked Nancy, nodded coolly to Cheryl, and followed Annelise down the driveway.

Eric stood up. "Uh, I guess I'd better . . . Hey, listen, I really am sorry about before."

"It's all right," Cheryl said. She sounded tired. "Let's forget about it, okay? But no more hiding out in bushes, agreed?"

"Agreed. I'll see you guys later."

He picked up his camera bag and headed for the driveway.

"I do like Eric, you know," Cheryl said after he'd left. "He gets carried away sometimes, but his heart's in the right place. Not like some of the people I run into."

"What about that guy Ramsay?" Nancy asked. "He didn't exactly act friendly to you."

Cheryl looked down at her hands, which were clasped in her lap. "Yeah, well . . ." she began. "It's hard to explain, but at meets, things happen a lot faster than in ordinary life." She sighed. "I met Ramsay a few months ago at an invitational meet in New York State. Zap! By the end of the first day, it was like we'd been going steady for months. But by the end of the meet, it was over. I don't know why, it just was—for me, anyway. Ramsay had trouble accepting it, but that's just the way it was. He's still pretty bitter about it."

Nancy frowned. "How bitter?" she asked. "Bitter enough to try to get back at you?"

44

"Ramsay?" Cheryl stared at her incredulously. "Oh, no. He might make a few remarks now and then, but he'd never try to hurt me. I'm sure of it!"

Nancy handed cups of fruit punch to George and Bess, then filled another for herself.

"This is quite a sight," George said, looking around the ballroom of the River Heights Country Club. Athletes and their host families milled about the spacious room, eating, talking, and dancing. A sumptuous buffet table with punch and soft drinks at one end of it had been set up along one wall of the room.

"It sure is." Bess sighed. Her blue eyes trailed longingly after a tall, muscular young man. "Some of these guys are incredibly gorgeous!"

George rolled her eyes at her cousin. "Do you realize that a lot of the people you're looking at are probably going to win medals at the next Olympics?"

"I realize I'm looking at some real hunks," Bess retorted. "Who cares about their medals? Come on, let's go meet a few of them."

Nancy smiled to herself as they walked away. George and Bess might be cousins and best friends, but they never seemed to see things the same way.

"Good evening, Nancy."

Nancy looked around, and when she saw the

45

white-haired man who had spoken to her, she smiled. "Oh, hi, Mr. Hornby," she said. "How are you?"

Lionel Hornby was vice-president of one of the banks in River Heights. Seeing him at the reception reminded Nancy that he was also chairman of the committee that had organized the games.

"I'm splendid," he said. He gestured toward the center of the ballroom. "What a fine bunch of young people! We read too much in the papers about the problems and not enough about the healthy, wholesome side of our town. I expect the games to be a real boost to River Heights."

Nancy wondered briefly if she should tell him about the harassment against Cheryl and Marta, but she didn't want to alarm Mr. Hornby— especially since he was feeling so positive about the games. Until she had a solid case to present, she decided, it would be wiser not to say anything at all.

"Well, enjoy yourself, Nancy. And please give my regards to your father." With a wave, Mr. Hornby vanished into the crowd.

Nancy started to look around the ballroom for Bess and George but was momentarily distracted when a flash went off in her face. She blinked, then saw that Barbara Williams was heading her way. Behind her was a short blond man with a camera.

"Was that somebody important?" Barbara asked, approaching Nancy.

"Mr. Hornby? He heads up the committee for the games," Nancy said.

"Really?" Barbara took out a pad and pen. The flash went off again as the blond man with the camera got another shot of Mr. Hornby.

"Who's that?" Nancy asked.

"Who, Steve Bukowski? He's here from Chicago to cover the games. It's part of some big photo contest. He doesn't know his way around town yet, so we agreed to help each other out."

Barbara cleared her throat, then went on in an official-sounding voice. "Tell me, Nancy, did Mr. Hornby ask you to investigate the mysterious incidents that have been taking place here at the International High School Games?"

Something about Barbara's tone of voice made Nancy look at her more closely. She was wearing a black skirt, a turquoise silk blouse, and a loose jacket that matched her skirt. There was an unusual, bulky-looking brooch pinned to her left lapel, and Nancy was pretty sure that it concealed a tiny microphone that was probably connected to a micro recorder in an inside pocket. Barbara was wired!

"Sorry, no comment," Nancy said. The flash went off again. "Excuse me," she added. "There's somebody I have to speak to."

47

"Wait," Barbara said as Nancy walked away. "I wanted to ask—"

Nancy pretended not to hear. Barbara might just be doing her job, but it was getting in the way of Nancy doing *her* job. How could she investigate the case if people kept interrupting her?

She edged through the crowd, keeping an eye out for Marta, Helga, Ramsay, and Cheryl. So far the evening had passed without incident.

Soon Nancy found herself next to one of the glass doors that opened onto the terrace. Light filtered through the doors, throwing an inviting circle of warm light onto the shadowy terrace. Nancy was thinking of stepping out for a breath of fresh air when she saw Cheryl walk by outside, followed a few moments later by Willy.

The light from the ballroom barely reached them as they met at the edge of the terrace. After a short embrace, they started hand-in-hand down a flight of stone steps that led to a lower terrace.

Nancy smiled to herself. Cheryl hadn't been kidding when she told Nancy that romances blossomed fast at these events.

Just then a furtive movement outside caught Nancy's eye. Someone was creeping down the steps after Willy and Cheryl. The slim white oval of a face in profile shone dimly for a moment as the follower glanced back toward the building. Then he or she was lost to the darkness.

Nancy did not hesitate. Slipping through the

door, she ran on tiptoe across the upper terrace, then paused at the head of the stairs to listen and to allow her eyes to adjust to the dark. She thought she heard the murmur of voices from somewhere below, but otherwise the night was quiet and still.

She crept down the steps to the lower level, then paused to get her bearings. Gradually, she began to pick out shapes in the darkness— tables, chairs, folded sun umbrellas. Near the edge of the terrace she could barely make out the silhouettes of two people sitting very close to each other. They were talking in low tones.

Nancy's breath caught in her chest when she caught sight of a third silhouette, not far from the couple, leaning forward as if about to spring!

Trying not to make any noise, Nancy began to run toward them, but her foot caught the leg of a misplaced chair, sending it clattering to the paving stones.

"Who's that?" came Willy's voice.

Footsteps ran in Nancy's direction, and instinctively she spread her arms to block the person's escape. Whoever was running must have been able to see her in the darkness, however, because the footsteps suddenly stopped. Metal scraped on the paving, and Nancy sensed, more than saw, the chair being raised high to smash her to the ground!

6

Danger at Dawn

The chair came whistling toward Nancy's head. Making a lightning-fast dive, she rolled to the side, and the chair crashed to the ground just to her left.

Before her assailant could try again, Nancy lashed out with her feet, striking a solid blow that caused her attacker to let out a yelp of pain. But before Nancy could get up, her assailant turned and raced toward the steps.

"Hey, what is this?" Willy shouted. "What is happening there?"

"Sounds like a fight," Nancy heard Cheryl say. "Come on!"

Nancy sprang to her feet just as Cheryl and Willy ran up to her.

"Who is that?" Willy demanded, grabbing Nancy's arm. "What is going on?"

"It's me, Nancy. Somebody just attacked me." She pulled free and started toward the clubhouse, but the person who had attacked her was already out of sight. "Too late." She let out a sigh of disappointment. She checked herself for injury, but other than some scratches and a soiled dress, she was okay.

"Who was it?" asked Cheryl. "And what were you doing here, anyway?"

"Right after you went outside, I noticed someone follow you down here," Nancy explained. "I didn't like the look of it, so I followed him." Recalling the assailant's high voice, she added, "Or her. When I made a noise, the person turned to run, but I was in the way."

"I thought I saw someone swing a chair," Willy said.

"Uh-huh. Luckily I was able to duck out of the way," Nancy said.

"Are you okay?" asked Cheryl, a worried look in her brown eyes. "Did you get hurt?"

Nancy shrugged. "A few scrapes, that's all. I should go wash up, though. I must be a mess."

"Do you want me to come with you?" Cheryl asked.

"No, thanks. I'm fine," Nancy replied. "But I think you two had better get back inside. I doubt whoever it was will try anything there."

As Nancy headed to the ladies room, she looked carefully around her. She had a suspicion she knew who the attacker was. When she came out of the ladies room, she ran into George, who took one shocked look at her scraped hands and rumpled dress, and asked, "What happened to you?"

"You should see the other guy," Nancy quipped. "I'll fill you in later, George. Right now I want to see if I can locate someone."

"Oh, look," George said in a low voice as she and Nancy walked through the ballroom. "Those must be the Johannsen twins. They're both world-class sprinters from Denmark."

Nancy followed George's gaze and saw two tall, lanky blond guys with nearly identical features. "Do they compete against each other?" she asked.

"Sometimes," George said. "But usually they divide up the events. The story is that they train by chasing each other around their dad's farm." She laughed, then said, "There's Marta. I hope she's feeling okay. She's awfully pale. That weird phone call this afternoon really shook her up."

Nancy looked in the blond girl's direction. She saw immediately what she was looking for: there was a red mark on Marta's shin that looked as if she had bumped into something—or been kicked.

As George and Nancy drew near, the German girl met Nancy's gaze, and Nancy thought she detected a look of fright on her face. Then Marta turned abruptly and headed in the direction of the ladies room.

Nancy started after her but stopped when she felt a hand on her arm.

"Hi, guys," Cheryl said. "Are you all recovered, Nancy?"

"Pretty much so," Nancy replied. "Listen— I—"

"Well, I don't know if I am," Cheryl interrupted. "I know this is a huge drag, Nancy, but would you mind driving me back to the house? After all that's happened today, I need my sleep. Besides, I want to go out real early tomorrow and check out the track."

Nancy hesitated, but the tired look on Cheryl's face decided her. She would have to wait until morning to confront Marta about the attack. "Sure, no problem," Nancy said. "How early is real early?"

Cheryl laughed. "What time does the sun come up? No, I'm exaggerating. I usually get up at around six. But don't worry, I don't expect you to take me to the track. If you show me the route on my map, I'm sure I'll be able to find my way there on my own."

As they turned to go, Eric called, "Hold it— great!" Nancy blinked when the flash went off, and when she opened her eyes, she found herself looking directly into Helga's intent gaze.

Nancy thought fast. Helga was certainly close

enough to have overheard Cheryl's plans. If she told Marta, and if Marta had been about to do something to Cheryl when Nancy interrupted her on the terrace, Marta might try again.

And what better setting for mischief than an empty running track at dawn?

The alarm buzzed, and Nancy reached her hand out and groped around on her bedside table until she found her clock. She turned off the alarm and held the clock near her face to see the time. Six o'clock. Right on schedule.

Quickly and silently, she got out of bed and dressed. Within minutes, she heard the door to the guest room open and close. Nancy waited until Cheryl had left the house. Then, grabbing a pair of binoculars, she headed for her car.

The drive to River Heights High took less than five minutes, even though Nancy had gone a roundabout way so that Cheryl wouldn't see her. Rather than use the parking lot, Nancy left her car on a nearby side street, then walked across the campus to the athletic field.

It was a beautiful day. The air still held a slight chill, but the sun would soon dry the dew on the grass. Nancy shaded her eyes against the glare and scanned the field. At first it looked empty, but then she glimpsed someone ducking behind the far corner of the bleachers.

She craned her neck for a better look, but the

person was now out of sight, and she didn't have time to go searching. Cheryl might arrive at any moment.

Nancy climbed the stands to the announcer's booth. From there, she could see the whole field and still stay out of sight. She didn't want to make Cheryl any more uneasy than she already was. Besides, there was still the possibility that Cheryl herself was somehow involved in the case. She might be using this time to set a trap for Marta.

A dot appeared at the entrance to the field. Lifting her binoculars to her eyes, Nancy focused on the dot. It was Cheryl, riding Nancy's ten-speed bike. She rode up to the foot of the stands, propped the bike against a bench, and sat down on the grass to do some stretches.

Nancy's gaze was distracted by a flash of light being reflected from the opposite end of the track. She brought the binoculars back up to her eyes and saw Eric half-hidden by the wall at the end of the stands. He was aiming a long telephoto lens at Cheryl.

Cheryl had been pretty steamed after he'd scared them in the Drews' backyard the day before. Eric was probably trying to stay out of her way to avoid making her mad again. Still, Nancy would have to keep an eye on him, just in case.

Looking back at the field, Nancy saw that Cheryl was upright now, propping each ankle in turn on the front wall of the stands and bending over to touch her forehead to her knee. Nancy shook her head. She considered herself to be in pretty good shape, but hanging around people like Cheryl was starting to make her feel downright lazy.

Cheryl finished her stretches, took off the jacket of her warm-up suit, and started down the track at an easy, loping pace.

Raising the binoculars again, Nancy swept the entire field from left to right, then back again. Eric was still there, taking pictures, but otherwise the area was empty and peaceful.

Nancy glanced back at Cheryl just in time to see the runner trip and go sprawling face first onto the cinder track. After a moment, she pushed herself up onto her knees and started to examine the track. Nancy saw her look down at something in her hands, then around at the stadium, as if she was expecting to see somebody there. Nancy was relieved that she didn't look injured.

Nancy got to her feet. She was about to go down to help Cheryl when she noticed some movement under the bleachers at the near end of the field. Focusing her binoculars on the spot, she saw that a person—no, two people—were crouched beneath the stands.

Leaving her binoculars in the announcer's booth, Nancy moved down the bleachers as quickly and quietly as she could. But by the time she reached the spot where the two people had been lurking, they had slipped away. A second later, Nancy spotted them walking quickly away from the field in the direction of the gate. She immediately recognized Barbara Williams and Steve Bukowski, the photographer who had been with Barbara at the River Heights Country Club the night before.

"Hey," Nancy called. "Wait up, I want to talk to you!"

They didn't look back, only walked more quickly. Nancy broke into a run, and they, too, began to run.

"Oh, no, you don't," Nancy muttered. With a fresh burst of speed, she closed the distance between them and launched herself at Barbara.

7

A Lost Clue

Barbara cried out as Nancy tackled her to the ground. "Let go of me! What are you doing?"

Barbara struggled up into a sitting position and glared at Nancy. A few steps away, Steve was staring at the two of them, a look of total astonishment on his face.

Nancy got to her feet. "Funny," she said. "I was just about to ask you the same question. Why were you hiding under the bleachers just now?"

"That's none of your business," Barbara said. She peered down at the bulky brooch pinned to her blazer. "If you broke my microcassette recorder, you're in big trouble."

"I'll take that chance," Nancy told her. "Let me guess. Somebody tipped you off that you'd get a big story about Cheryl Pierce if you came here this morning to watch her train."

Barbara didn't answer, but her expression told Nancy that she was right.

"Then, when you saw her fall," Nancy went on, "you realized that the big story was her so-called accident. But your presence here meant that it wasn't an accident, and you were afraid that might look suspicious. So you tried to get away without anyone seeing you. How am I doing so far?"

"We have as much right to be here as you do," Steve said. He was about to say something more, but Barbara motioned him to be quiet.

"I'm not denying your right to be here," Nancy told them. "But if somebody laid a trap for Cheryl, and you had advance knowledge of it and didn't warn her, that makes you accessories to the crime."

Nancy knew her words sounded harsh, but she had to make Barbara and Steve understand how serious the situation was. "Please, it's very important that you tell me everything."

Barbara and Steve exchanged a nervous look, and finally Barbara said, "Okay, I got an anonymous tip to be here this morning. But it wasn't the way you think. Nothing was said about Cheryl getting hurt. I thought I was going to find out that she was doing something dishonest."

Nancy nodded. She had thought of that possibility, too. "How did you get this tip?" she asked.

"I found a note in my jacket pocket when I got home from the reception last night."

"May I see it? Do you have it with you?"

"No, I'm afraid . . ." Barbara hesitated, and her face turned pink. "Well, I burned it."

Nancy stared at her, unbelieving. "You did *what?*"

"I burned it," she repeated apologetically. "A reporter has a duty to protect her sources."

"Do you remember what the note looked like?" Nancy asked. "Was it typed? Handwritten? What kind of paper?"

"It was just an ordinary piece of white paper, sort of glossy, with a scribbled note in pencil."

"Too bad you burned it," Nancy mused out loud. "Handwriting is hard to disguise, and glossy paper is the best kind for lifting prints." She looked back over her shoulder toward the track, then said, "Well, thanks for your help. I'd better go see how Cheryl is."

"We'll come, too," Barbara said. "I'll feel awful if she's hurt."

The three of them walked back onto the field and found Cheryl still standing near where she had fallen, talking to Eric. Nancy approached them quickly, with Barbara and Steve not far behind her.

Cheryl glanced over her shoulder, saw Nancy, and said, "I was just talking about you, Nancy.

This is getting serious. Somebody just tried to break my neck. Look at this!"

She held out her hand and showed Nancy a length of transparent nylon fishing line.

"It was stretched across the track at ankle height," Cheryl added. "If I'd been running full out, instead of warming up, I could have been badly hurt." She paused and glanced at Barbara and Steve. "What are they doing here?"

Nancy quickly told her about the anonymous tip.

Barbara put her hand in her jacket pocket, and Nancy was pretty sure she was turning on her microcassette recorder. "I noticed you fell a few minutes ago while warming up," the reporter said to Cheryl. "Did that have anything to do with the harassment people are talking about?"

Barbara's concern for Cheryl sounded genuine, Nancy thought, but she obviously wasn't concerned enough to respect Cheryl's privacy. Could it be that Barbara's interest went beyond just wanting to get a scoop?

"I couldn't tell you," Cheryl replied, obviously annoyed.

"Hey, let her alone," Eric said suddenly. He stepped in front of Steve, who had just raised his camera and aimed it at Cheryl.

"Why? You have an exclusive contract?" Steve demanded. "This is a public place, you know. I have a right."

61

"You don't have any right to harass people," Eric insisted. "And that's exactly what you're doing."

Steve sidestepped him and said, "Let's ask her. Cheryl, am I harassing you?"

"Look, I came out here to be alone," Cheryl said, "not to have people fighting over me. The meet starts in a couple of hours, and I want to be calm and together for it. So if you'll all excuse me—"

"Do you want a lift back to the house?" Nancy offered sympathetically.

"Thanks, but I'd rather use the bike—as long as no one tags along and bugs me, that is." Cheryl looked sharply at Barbara and Steve and started across to the bleachers, where she had left her jacket and the bike. A few moments later, she rode out the gate.

"We'd better get moving, too," Barbara said to Steve. "Listen, Nancy, I'm sorry if I got angry before. I'm not used to having people tackle me, that's all. Can we get together later on? I'd love to hear your ideas about this harassment business."

And tape them, Nancy added to herself. Aloud, she said, "That's a great idea, Barbara. I'll see what I can do."

Once Barbara and Steve were out of earshot, Nancy turned to Eric and asked, "What were *you* doing here at six-thirty in the morning?"

"Taking pictures of Cheryl, of course." His raised eyebrows hinted that Nancy was crazy for even asking the question.

"But how did you know she would be here this early?" she pressed.

Eric shrugged. "I heard her mention it to you last night, at the party. Besides, Cheryl usually looks over the track first thing on the morning of a meet."

"When did you get here?"

"A little after you and a little before Cheryl," he replied with a grin. "I saw you climbing up into the announcer's booth."

Nancy sighed. She had hoped that Eric might have arrived early enough to get a glimpse of whoever had tied the nylon trip wire across the track.

"I'd better get moving," she said. "See you later."

Nancy climbed up to the announcer's booth to retrieve her binoculars, then headed for her car. She pulled into her driveway just as Cheryl was walking the bike into the garage.

"Hi," Cheryl called, emerging from the garage. She seemed to have regained her good spirits. "I'm starved."

"Me, too," Nancy replied. "Let's see what we can find to eat."

The girls were just sitting down to a breakfast

of granola topped with raisins and fresh sliced strawberries when the phone rang. Nancy glanced at her watch, then grabbed the receiver.

It was George. "Nancy," she said in an urgent voice, "this is getting serious. Marta got another threatening phone call about ten minutes ago. She's been hysterical ever since. Helga is starting to wonder if she should call a doctor."

"Same kind of call as yesterday?" asked Nancy.

"I guess so," George replied. "I didn't hear this one."

"Too bad," Nancy said. "By the way, where was Marta before the call?"

George hesitated. "Out for a run, I guess. She and Helga were both gone by the time I woke up. I thought they were together, but I guess not, because Marta got back a few minutes earlier than Helga."

"Hmm," said Nancy. She glanced at her watch again. "I don't have time to come over before we go to the games. You'll just have to do your best to calm them down, and we'll go over everything later. I'll see you at the games, okay?"

She hung up the telephone and walked slowly back to the kitchen table. The case was getting more confusing every minute. New attempts had been made to sabotage both Cheryl and Marta, and both girls had a reason to want the other out of the competition. Marta and Helga had both

64

been out of the Faynes' house early enough to have set the wire. And Cheryl could easily have stopped at a phone booth on her way home to make that second threatening call to Marta; that might explain her renewed good mood. So far, it certainly seemed as though they were trying to sabotage each other.

Nancy drummed her fingers on the kitchen table, concentrating. Somehow it seemed too neat. And then there were the reporters and photographers. How did they fit in?

"Nancy?" said Cheryl. Her voice sounded loud, as if she had already spoken three or four times without any response.

Nancy blinked. "Sorry, what is it?"

"I was wondering if you have a bathing suit I could borrow," Cheryl said. "We're about the same size, I think."

"I guess so. Why?"

"They announced yesterday that the high school pool will be open for us during the games," Cheryl explained. "I thought I'd take advantage of it. There's nothing like a few fast laps to soothe you and cool you off."

Nancy nodded. "I'm sure I can come up with something," she said.

"Bring one for yourself, too," Cheryl called as Nancy started up the stairs. "I love to have company when I swim."

* * *

Nancy dropped Cheryl off at the locker room and strolled over to the athletic field. The stands were already starting to fill up with spectators, and the athletes were gathering on the grass near one end of the stands, waiting for the opening parade.

Nancy walked in their direction. She had been hoping to talk to Marta that morning—about the second phone call *and* about the previous night's attack—but so far she hadn't seen the German girl or her trainer.

As Nancy approached the athletes, Willy waved and called to her. Annelise was standing next to him.

"Good morning," he said, smiling, as Nancy came over. "What a beautiful day, isn't it?"

"It sure is," Nancy replied, glancing around her. "Hi, Annelise. Are you enjoying your visit to River Heights so far?"

"Yes," the Swiss girl said. "It is very nice here."

"Can you tell me about the history of your town?" Willy asked Nancy. "The history of America interests me very much."

"I can tell you a little, I think," Nancy said. She searched her mind for some of the local history she had had to learn in grade school. "Let's see—"

"Attention, please," a loud voice rang out, and Nancy turned to see a man in a blue satin

66

windbreaker who was speaking into a bullhorn. "Will the athletes please take their places for the opening parade."

"Excuse me," Willy said. He and Annelise moved over to where the other athletes were lining up. Just then Cheryl came jogging over, on her way back from the gym. She took her place among the other athletes, wearing a very solemn expression. This moment clearly meant a lot to her.

There was a stir in the crowd, and Helga Roth appeared, holding the arm of the official in the blue windbreaker. She was talking rapidly, and although her voice was too low for Nancy to hear her words, Helga's whole body conveyed a sense of urgent intensity. The official listened, shook his head, then listened some more.

From the loudspeakers came the opening music of a lively march. The athletes straightened their ranks, and as the first of the competitors stepped out onto the track, the spectators began to cheer.

But at that moment, Helga shouted, "There! Cheryl Pierce—she is the one!"

8

A Serious Charge

At the sound of her name, Cheryl stopped so abruptly that the young woman behind her in line almost tripped over her.

"Excuse me, miss," the man in the blue windbreaker said to Cheryl. He took her arm and led her out of the line. "Would you mind coming with me, please?"

Nancy moved closer so she could hear.

Cheryl stared at the man, then looked back at the parading athletes. Over half the athletes were already out on the field.

"What is it?" Cheryl asked. "Can't it wait?"

"I'm sorry," the man said. "Questions have been raised that may affect your eligibility to participate in the games. Until they're settled . . ."

Cheryl's jaw dropped. "Eligibility? What do

you mean? Are you trying to say you're disqualifying me?" She sounded completely bewildered.

Nancy glanced around. Not far away, Barbara
was pulling her microcassette recorder from her
jacket pocket. Behind her, Nancy heard the
familiar click-whirr of a camera—Eric's. Helga
remained just a few steps away, watching and
listening closely.

The last of the entrants were marching onto the
field, and Nancy saw that Marta was among them.
The German girl looked over at Cheryl and the
official with an expression that seemed to be
somewhere between frightened and sly.

"I am not disqualifying you," the official said.
He glanced around uncomfortably at Barbara,
Nancy, and Eric. "It's simply that—look, hadn't
we better talk this over in private?"

"Away from my friends, you mean?" Cheryl
said. "Sorry, but no way. Whatever you've got
to say to me, you can tell me right here and
now."

"Very well, young lady," the official said. "According to Ms. Roth, your conduct yesterday and
today has been totally unsportsmanlike. She says
that you have deliberately harassed your rival
Marta Schmidt to the extent of making threatening phone calls to her. I'm sorry, but we simply
cannot overlook that sort of behavior."

"And you took her word for it, without any
proof?" Cheryl asked.

"Ms. Roth is an Olympic medalist," the man replied stiffly.

"And I'm just some kid you've never heard of, is that it?"

"Hello, Robert," came a deep voice. "What's the problem here?"

Nancy glanced over and recognized Lionel Hornby, the chairman of the games committee.

"Mr. Hornby," the official in the windbreaker said. He stepped over to Hornby, and the two men spoke for a moment in low, guarded tones.

After a few minutes, Hornby looked around. "Ah—Ms. Roth?" Helga stepped forward, and they spoke for a minute or two longer. Helga seemed to become agitated.

Finally Hornby nodded. "I see," he said calmly. "And I understand your concern. You may be sure that I shall do all I can to deal with the matter."

Helga did not look satisfied, but she seemed to realize that she had reached a dead end. When she stepped away from the two men, she turned to glare at Cheryl and Nancy.

Hornby walked over to Cheryl. "Ms. Pierce?" he said. "I'm sorry you're missing the opening parade. Ms. Roth has made some serious charges, you understand. We have to look into them carefully. We may need to ask you some questions later on. In the meantime, I hope you enjoy your participation in the games."

"You mean I can go?" asked Cheryl, looking relieved.

Hornby nodded and said pleasantly, "That's right. And I hope you'll forgive this misunderstanding."

Cheryl turned and looked daggers at Helga. "Some people I'm going to find hard to forgive," she said in an icy voice.

As Cheryl walked toward the field, Hornby caught Nancy's eye and motioned with his head for her to join him.

"What's the story here, Nancy?" he demanded. She quickly filled him in on what had been happening, and as she spoke his face grew more and more grave.

"This is terrible!" he exclaimed when she had finished. "Why didn't you say something to me before this?"

"I realize now that I should have," Nancy admitted.

Hornby shook his head slowly. "We have to stop this before it destroys the games. Nancy, will you try to get to the bottom of all this and find the person responsible? You'd be doing a big favor for everyone who's worked so hard to bring the games to River Heights and make them a success."

"Of course, Mr. Hornby," Nancy replied.

Hornby took out one of his business cards, wrote something on the back of it, and handed it to her. "This is a note instructing anyone connected with the games to cooperate fully with you," he said. "If there's any difficulty, ask the person to speak to me. And good luck."

The opening parade had come to an end, and the competitors had scattered. Those whose events were early on the day's schedule were warming up, while the rest watched and talked among themselves.

Nancy found George and Bess near the shot-put area, where the first round was about to begin. Ramsay Roberts, the red-haired Canadian Nancy had met the day before, noticed her arrival and waved. She waved back.

"Nancy," Bess said in a low voice, "you've been holding out on us! Who is that gorgeous hunk?"

"His name is Ramsay," Nancy replied with a laugh. "He's a shot-putter from Canada. And now you know just about as much as I do."

"I want to know more," Bess sighed. "*Much* more. It's not very far to Canada, after all."

"Far enough," George said matter-of-factly. She watched Ramsay for a moment. "Hmm— he's got pretty good form. I'll be surprised if he doesn't place." Turning to Nancy, she asked, "What was that commotion at the start of the parade? Cheryl looked pretty unhappy."

Nancy told them about the confrontation between Helga and Cheryl, and about Mr. Hornby asking her to investigate. "I can't waste any time, either," she continued. "The way the incidents are escalating, I'm afraid somebody is going to get seriously hurt before long."

"Do you have any suspects?" asked Bess.

Nancy rolled her eyes. "Plenty," she replied. "But first I have to figure out exactly who is the real target of these incidents. If it *is* Cheryl, then Marta and Helga are obvious suspects, and the so-called threatening calls are just a smoke screen."

"I saw Marta's face this morning," George said, "and I can tell you she wasn't faking. She was definitely scared out of her wits by that call."

"Okay," Nancy agreed. "But Helga could still have made the call herself, without Marta's knowledge. In fact, if Helga is behind the harassment, I would bet that she'd be very careful to protect Marta by keeping her in the dark."

"I guess, but— Oh, wait, your Canadian friend over there is about to make his first put."

Ramsay Roberts walked up to the cinder-covered shot-put circle. Holding the twelve-pound, brass-covered shot easily in his right hand, he stood at the rear of the circle. He brought his hand to his shoulder, and with the shot in his upturned palm, nestled the shot against his neck.

"I wish I had a camera," Bess whispered.

"Shh!" hissed George. "He's winding up."

In what seemed like slow motion, the Canadian athlete balanced on one foot and bent over so far that he looked as if he would topple. Suddenly, he whirled around and hurled the brass shot away, putting his arm, his shoulder, and his whole body into the motion. He seemed about to fall, but some fast footwork brought him upright, still inside the circle.

The spectators started to clap. The field judge who was measuring Ramsay's throw stood up and said, "Roberts, first put, sixty feet, four and three-quarters inches."

Bess turned to George. "Is that good?" she asked.

"You bet," George replied with an impressed nod. "At this level of competition, anything over fifty-five feet would probably place him in the top five."

Nancy had watched his performance in silence. Now she commented, "Ramsay seems to hold a real grudge against Cheryl. She told me they had a brief romance that didn't work out. And from what we know at this point, Ramsay could have been behind any of the incidents."

"No one with his looks could do anything like that," Bess said emphatically.

George rolled her eyes.

"The problem with this case," Nancy went on, "is that I have too many suspects. Besides Helga and Marta, there's Barbara, for instance. She may have been at the track this morning because she got an anonymous tip, as she said. But she and her friend Steve could have put up that trip wire."

"You mean, if there's no news, make some?" George said.

"I've heard of that happening. Hurting someone just to make a hot story is pretty extreme," Nancy agreed, "but that means Eric's also in the running as a suspect."

As the girls were waiting for the next shot-putter, Cheryl and Willy walked over to them. "Hi," Cheryl said to Nancy. "I was looking for you. Willy and I both have some time before our next events, so we're going for a swim. Want to come along?"

Nancy quickly scanned the field. She had been keeping an eye out for Marta since the opening parade but hadn't seen her anywhere. "Okay," Nancy agreed. Whether Cheryl was a potential victim or a potential suspect, Nancy thought she should stay close to her. She turned to George and Bess. "What about you two? Feel like a swim?"

George shook her head. "I don't have a suit with me," she said.

"And I'm going to watch my houseguest, Marie-Laure, in the high jump," said Bess.

"All right," said Nancy. "I'll look for you after our swim."

As they walked toward the gym, Willy told Cheryl, "Annelise said she would meet us at the pool, but I do not think she will swim."

"Why not?" asked Cheryl.

Willy shrugged. "I do not know. I believe she was once a competitive swimmer, but something happened and she gave it up."

"I wonder why?" Cheryl said. "I can't imagine giving up running."

Eric caught up with them just outside the gym. "Mind if I come along?" he asked.

"If you want to," Cheryl replied with a shrug.

Nancy and Cheryl changed into their suits in the locker room, and Nancy led the way to the indoor pool. A dozen or so athletes were already taking advantage of the chance for a swim. Willy was standing near the entrance, talking to Annelise. He waved to Cheryl, who smiled and waved back. Then, suddenly, her smile froze on her face.

Nancy followed Cheryl's gaze. Marta and Helga were standing at one end of the pool.

The stony expression still on her face, Cheryl walked slowly to the opposite end of the pool from where Helga and Marta were. Nancy followed her. Cheryl pulled off her sweatshirt and dropped it, along with her towel, on one of the benches. She paced off six feet from the end of the pool, took a couple of deep breaths, then sprinted forward and launched herself into the air in a perfect racing dive.

At that instant, every light in the pool room went out. A moment later, Nancy heard Cheryl's cry, followed by a loud splash.

9

Lights Out!

"Cheryl!" Willy was shouting in the suddenly blackened pool room. At first the only answer was more splashing sounds. Then the other athletes began calling out to one another, some in languages Nancy couldn't understand.

Nancy knew she had to turn the lights back on—fast. She tried to visualize the layout of the room. The light switches were probably near the double doors that led to the locker rooms. She made her way carefully along the wall to the left, moved forward until she reached a corner, then turned right. All the while, frantic splashing echoed in the darkness.

Finally, Nancy saw a dim light filtering in from the corridor. Hurrying over to the doors, she ran her hands along the tiled wall. Nothing on the right side, but on the left—

She flipped the bank of switches up and narrowed her eyes against the sudden glare. A quick glance at the out-of-the-way location of the switches told Nancy that it would have been just about impossible to turn the lights off accidentally. Her gaze then flew to the pool, where Willy was kneeling by the edge. He was stretching out his hand to a shaken Cheryl, who was breathing in huge gulps of air. The other athletes were crowding around, but Willy motioned them back.

"Give me room," he said. He helped Cheryl up onto the tiled edge of the pool. Eric, a few feet away, was snapping one photo after another.

"Where's Steve when I need him?" someone near Nancy muttered. She glanced over and saw Barbara writing hastily in a little notebook. Helga and Marta were standing where they had been, not far from the pool's edge, near the diving boards. Eric, with two cameras around his neck, stood off to one side, taking pictures. Annelise and some of the other athletes stood in a circle, talking in hushed voices.

"This didn't look like an accident, Nancy," Barbara said.

Nancy didn't think so, either. But once again, there were almost too many suspects to choose from. Somehow she had to narrow down the list.

"Do you mind telling me where you were standing when the lights went out?" Nancy asked Barbara.

"You've got to be kidding," Barbara returned. "You don't really think I had anything to do with this business, do you?"

"I was hoping you might have seen something, that's all," Nancy replied evenly.

"Sorry," Barbara told her. "I'm afraid I didn't see anything unusual."

Cheryl was on her feet when Nancy went over to her. "Are you all right?" Nancy asked.

"More or less," Cheryl said shakily. She rubbed a red mark on her left shoulder. "I must have hit the lane marker when I dived in. And I think I swallowed a couple of gallons of water. What happened, anyway?"

Nancy gave her a concerned glance. "Somebody flipped the switches," she said. "I'm afraid this wasn't an accident."

Cheryl's face tightened. She looked around the room and focused her gaze on Marta and Helga. Marta looked frightened, but Helga's face was closed and stern.

Reassured that Cheryl was all right, Nancy made her way back to the spot where she had been standing when the lights went out. She began to create a mental image of where everyone had been. Marta and Helga had been near the edge of the pool before the lights were turned off. Either of them might have had enough time to get to the switches, but Nancy had to admit to herself that she couldn't be sure of that. Her attention had been on Cheryl, not on the area near the door where the switches were. Willy and Annelise had also been present.

Still, the incident had narrowed the field of suspects a little. Ramsay Roberts was probably still out on the field. Unless he was conspiring with someone else, he was obviously innocent. And Cheryl herself could be crossed off the list. She couldn't have staged this incident, although it was still possible that she was responsible for the phone calls to Marta.

Cheryl started to walk over to the bench where she had left her towel and sweatshirt, but she stopped herself. "I came here to swim," she announced. "And that's what I'm going to do. What about you, Nancy?"

"I've changed my mind," Nancy replied. "I'll just watch." Something told her she should keep a sharp eye on things.

Nancy noticed that Marta had gotten into the pool and was doing slow laps. Cheryl apparently noticed at the same time, because a tight smile flashed across her face and she stepped over to a free lane right next to Marta's. She dove in, surfaced, and started down the length of the pool in a strong, fast crawl stroke. She drew even with Marta, then easily passed her. A moment later Marta noticed, and she picked up her stroke to keep pace with Cheryl.

By the time the two rivals drew close to the far

end of the pool, they were both swimming full-out. After a quick racing turn, they were on their way back to the end where Nancy was standing. Cheryl still held a lead, but Marta was narrowing it.

Everyone had stopped along the side of the pool to watch the match. Some of the athletes were cheering. Helga was shouting, too, but the flood of German sounded angry, not encouraging. Nancy couldn't tell if the anger was directed more at Cheryl or at Marta.

The two swimmers reached the point in front of Nancy at exactly the same instant. For one moment, Cheryl and Marta grinned at each other, but then the grins faded.

Helga, hands on hips, had come over and was talking sternly to Marta in German. Then she turned to Cheryl.

"You will never be a great athlete without self-control," Helga said. "You and Marta have an important contest this afternoon. You know this. It is the reason you came here. Yet you risk everything to put on a childish show. You should both be ashamed. Marta, come!"

Her face bright red, Marta climbed out of the pool and followed her trainer in the direction of the locker room.

Cheryl watched them silently, a sober, sheepish look on her face. Hoisting herself out of the pool, she walked over to the bench where Nancy sat.

"Helga's right," Cheryl confided, picking up her towel and drying off. "If my coach back at school had just seen what had happened, she'd probably suspend me from the track team. I guess I got carried away."

Nancy gave her a sympathetic look. "You've been under a lot of strain," she pointed out.

"A big meet is always a lot of pressure," Cheryl replied, rubbing her hair with the towel. "And it doesn't help to have to keep looking over my shoulder, wondering who's out to get me. But what if my dream comes true, and I get the chance to compete in the Olympics? There'd be hundreds of millions of people from every part of the world watching me. I'd have to be able to handle that."

She pulled on her sweatshirt and added, "No, Helga's right. I've got a lot of growing up to do."

Willy came over. "How are you feeling?" he asked.

"Wiped out," Cheryl told him. "But I'll get over it."

"I must go. The fifteen-hundred-meter run is coming up."

"But that's your best event," Cheryl wailed. "And I haven't been thinking about anything but me!"

Willy smiled. "Neither have I," he said. "But there's still plenty of time to warm up."

"Could I ask you a couple of questions before you go?" said Nancy.

"Oh, not right before his event," Cheryl exclaimed. "Can't it wait?"

Willy held up his hand. "It's all right, Cheryl." Then, turning to Nancy, he said, "You are trying to find the one responsible for all these accidents, yes? I will help however I can."

"Thanks," Nancy said. "Do you remember where you were standing when the lights went out?"

He furrowed his brow. "I think I was near the end of the bench, over there." He pointed. "Yes, that is right, I remember."

Nancy looked around and began to feel a slight stirring of hope. Anyone who wanted to get to the light switches from the pool area would have had to go past Willy first.

"Who was standing near you?" she continued.

"Ah, that is more difficult." He fell silent. Finally he said, "No, I am sorry. People were moving around so much. You understand."

"Do you recall seeing Marta? Helga?"

He shook his head, then said, "Wait, Marta I remember. I saw her at the edge of the pool before Cheryl started to dive."

"You're sure? Did you see which way she went?"

"That I cannot say." He frowned. "I think I wondered if she was leaving the pool, so she might have been toward the door. But I cannot be sure."

He glanced at his watch and added, "I am sorry, I really must go to the track to warm up."

"Thanks, you've been a great help," Nancy said. "And good luck in the fifteen hundred meters."

As Willy strode away, Cheryl turned to Nancy and said, "Marta's the one, isn't she? That innocent look of hers is a lie!"

"Well . . ." Nancy hesitated. "If Willy's recollection is right, it means that she could have turned off the lights. It doesn't mean that she *did*. A lot of other people were here, too. And whether Marta had a part in any of the other incidents, we just don't know."

"Maybe you don't," Cheryl said grimly, "but *I* do. And I'm not going to take it lying down!"

She pulled her sweatshirt over her head and stormed off toward the locker room. Nancy hurried after her. Mr. Hornby was counting on her to head off trouble, and right now Cheryl was like a bundle of dynamite looking for a place to explode.

Cheryl pushed through the locker-room doors, with Nancy right behind her. Inside they found Annelise sitting on a bench in front of an open locker whose door was beat up and dented. Annelise looked up, startled. She was in her shorts and jersey, and a folded pair of white warm-up pants was lying next to her on the bench.

"Have you seen Marta?" demanded Cheryl.

"She and Helga were here a few minutes ago," Annelise told her. "She changed into running clothes and left. I think you will find her at the track." She stood up and pulled on the white pants.

"Hey!" Cheryl said. "How'd you rate a fresh warm-up suit? You must know somebody!"

"It is so stupid," Annelise replied, looking embarrassed. "I spilled some juice on my pants. It is a guava juice I always drink when I am in training or competition, and it made a bright pink stain." She gestured toward the open locker. "I tried to get it off, but it looked dreadful. So I told the man in the supply room, and he gave me these new pants."

Cheryl nodded distractedly. "Well, I'd better change and get over to the track. I need to have a talk with someone."

She reached in the pocket of her sweatshirt for the key to her locker. "What—?" she murmured, pulling a piece of paper from her pocket.

"What is it?" Nancy asked.

Cheryl unfolded the paper, and the color drained from her face.

A second later, she handed the sheet to Nancy.

"Go home now," the note read, "before it's too late."

10

Marta's Confession

Nancy reread the threatening note, then asked, "This wasn't in your pocket before, was it?"

Cheryl blinked. "No, no. I would have found it when I dropped my locker key in, wouldn't I?" She fell silent for a moment, then burst out, "Who's doing this? Who's after me? I've never done anyone any harm. Why does somebody want to hurt me?"

"I don't know," Nancy admitted. "But I'm going to do everything I can to find out."

Holding the note by the corners, she studied it closely. The words in the message had apparently been cut from a glossy magazine. But what kind of magazine?

"What is it?" Cheryl asked.

"Nothing," said Nancy. "Not yet, at least. I wish I had a pair of tweezers with me."

"Tweezers?" Annelise asked. "One moment." She reached in her locker, withdrew a cosmetic bag, and rummaged around inside it. "Here," she said, holding out a pair of tweezers.

Nancy took them from Annelise. "Thanks."

With one blade of the tweezers, she carefully pried up the edge of "before," the longest word in the note, and peered at the underside. "I can make out what looks like part of a drawing of a cigarette," she announced. "The name of the brand starts with *W-e-e.* 'Wee'? I never heard of it."

"In Europe there is a brand of cigarettes called Weekend," Annelise said. "American words are very stylish in many European countries."

"That might be what it is," Nancy said thoughtfully. "If so, whoever constructed this note used words from a European magazine."

"But all the words are English," objected Cheryl. "Would you find them in a foreign magazine?"

"It might be from England," Nancy pointed out.

Annelise said, "Also, in Switzerland, we have magazines in English, you know." She sounded slightly offended. "Even very popular magazines, for men, for women, even for fans of sports. You will find magazines in English much more easily in Europe than I will find magazines in German or French here in your country."

89

"Oh, I'm sure you're right," Cheryl said hastily. "But doesn't that mean that whoever made this note must have brought the magazine from Europe?"

Nancy shook her head. "Not necessarily. I've seen some foreign magazines right here in River Heights. There are a few newsstands that sell them."

Nancy gave Annelise back her tweezers, then carefully folded the threatening note and put it in the side pocket of her gym bag. "I'll take a closer look later, when I get home," she explained. "Right now I want to go back to the track and ask some questions." She sighed. "I just wish I felt sure of getting answers."

Nancy showed her host family pass to the guard at the entrance to the field, and he waved her through. Bess spotted Nancy and came rushing over.

"Isn't it wonderful?" Bess exclaimed. "Marie-Laure placed in the preliminaries! That means she'll be in the finals tomorrow."

"That's great," Nancy said. She shot her friend a curious smile. She'd never seen Bess so enthusiastic about a sports event. Ordinarily, Bess's reaction was a politely suppressed yawn.

"Hey, is anything wrong?" Bess asked. "Anything new, I mean? I saw that girl who's staying with George a few minutes ago. She looked really upset."

Nancy raised her eyebrows. "Marta? Which way did she go? I want to ask her a few questions."

Bess waved down the field. "Over that way, I think. Listen, I'm going to go watch the discus throw, okay? What did you say that guy's name was, the Canadian? I'm planning to be his cheering section."

"Ramsay," Nancy told her with a laugh. "Ramsay Roberts. I'll see you later, Bess."

As she walked alongside the track, she heard the announcer give the last call for the 1500-meter run. That was Willy's event, she remembered. The competitors were gathered near the starting blocks, stripping off their warm-up suits. The starter and his assistant had taken up their positions on either side of the track. A whistle blast sounded from the judges at the finish line, and Willy and the seven others moved onto the track and stood near their starting blocks.

"Runners," the starter shouted, "to your marks!" He raised a pistol over his head. The runners crouched down with one knee on the surface of the track, leaning forward so that part of their weight was on their hands.

"Set!"

They pushed themselves up into a position that

looked impossibly hard to hold. At last, the sharp pop of the pistol rang out, and the runners exploded off the starting blocks.

"Pretty impressive, isn't it?" came a voice.

Nancy looked around and found herself face-to-face with Barbara.

"Watching these guys makes me feel a little guilty for being such a creampuff," the reporter added.

Nancy smiled but didn't say anything.

"Listen," Barbara said. "I want to help you on your case. And not just because it might make a terrific story. I saw what happened back at the pool. Whoever's doing this stuff has to be stopped before someone gets badly hurt."

"I agree," Nancy said. "But—"

"You're thinking about this morning, aren't you? But I really didn't know what was going to happen. If I had, I would have warned Cheryl." She looked earnestly into Nancy's face. "Okay, so you don't trust me," she said. "I can't really blame you. But I'm going to see what I can dig up just the same. And if I get anything useful, I'll pass it on to you. Deal?"

Barbara was right. Nancy *didn't* trust her. Except for pushing Cheryl off the stands, Barbara had been nearby every time Cheryl had had an accident. She could easily have made the calls to Marta, too, and she certainly seemed willing to go to a lot of trouble to get a good story. Nancy had no proof, but maybe Barbara herself would provide some. As long as Nancy kept a careful eye on her, it might be helpful if the reporter thought that she and Nancy were on the same side.

"Deal," Nancy told her.

Turning her attention back to the track, Nancy saw that the runners were rounding the last turn and entering the homestretch. Willy wasn't in the lead, she could see that. But as the pack drew closer, she spotted him in third or fourth place.

"Go, Willy!" she shouted. *"Go!"*

He couldn't possibly have heard her amid all the cheering, but he seemed to put on an extra spurt of speed a moment later. In the last few yards he drew almost level with the runner in second place. From where she was standing, Nancy couldn't tell whether he actually passed him or not, but at the very least he had come in third. That would guarantee him a spot in the finals.

"Whew!" Nancy let out the breath she had been holding and tried to shake some of the tension out of her shoulders. When George had asked if she would be one of the hosts for the athletes, she had agreed, but she hadn't expected to become so involved in the competitions.

"Okay, I'll catch you later," Barbara said. "Wish me luck."

"Sure, Barbara," Nancy replied with a smile. And I'll double-check any facts you give me, she added to herself.

As Nancy turned away, she saw Marta a few feet away. The German girl was staring to her left with a desolate look on her face. Nancy followed the direction of Marta's gaze and saw Willy talking to some of the other competitors from the 1500-meter run.

Marta—and Willy? Nancy snapped her fingers. Of course! She strode quickly over to Marta and said, "That was you at the country club last night, wasn't it?"

Marta's blue eyes widened. "I was at the country club, yes," she said carefully. "We all were."

"You saw Cheryl and Willy taking a walk on the terrace," Nancy pressed. "You followed them. I saw you. What were you planning to do? Simply spy on them? Or attack them with a chair, the way you attacked me?"

"I . . . I . . . This is madness! What are you saying?" Marta backed away defensively. "I would never do such things to Willy! I love Willy!"

Marta gasped, and her hand flew to her mouth. Her eyes filled with tears, and a look of misery came over her face. "Yes, I followed them," she said after a long pause. "But not to hurt them.

94

Just to know for sure that it was over. And then someone came—I didn't know it was you—and I was so ashamed, so afraid to be discovered, that I—"

"What is this here?" Helga came rushing over, wedged herself in front of Nancy, and took Marta by the shoulders. After a stream of rapid-fire German directed at Marta, Helga turned on Nancy.

"This is not correct!" she exclaimed. "You are clearly part of this conspiracy to upset Marta and make her lose. But it will not be allowed to continue. I am going this moment to file a report with the chairman of the games. Marta, come!"

Marta gave Nancy a pleading look, then turned and followed her trainer.

Nancy watched in frustration as Helga and Marta made their way through the crowd. She had finally managed to talk to Marta, only to be interrupted. Nancy knit her brow in concentration. Had Marta been on the point of saying something important when Helga interrupted?

A voice calling her name interrupted Nancy's thoughts.

From the middle of the field, Cheryl waved and called out again, "Nancy," then came over to her. "I've been looking for you," she said. "Did you watch Willy's race? Wasn't he terrific?"

For a moment, Nancy thought that perhaps

Cheryl's excitement about Willy had overcome her worry about the accidents and the threatening note. Then Cheryl's expression darkened.

"Listen, I hate to ask you this," Cheryl went on, frowning, "but would you mind taking me back to the house for a minute? Some lowlife took my lunch from my gym bag. It's only a can of protein drink, but it's the only lunch I eat on days when I'm competing. Look, I refuse to let these pranks get in the way of my performance. If you don't mind, I'd really like to pick up another one."

"I'd be glad to," Nancy told her. "But are you sure you have time? Aren't you racing soon?"

Cheryl shook her head. "I'm in the last heat," she said. "I still have plenty of time, and my stomach is really starting to complain."

"Okay, let's go."

The parking lot was nearly full, but Nancy managed to ease her Mustang out of its slot without scraping the next car. Leaving the parking lot, she turned onto the side street that bordered the athletic field.

Suddenly a battered station wagon pulled away from the curb, right in front of her. Nancy jammed her foot on the brake pedal, then gasped in horror as the pedal sank straight to the floor.

She had no brakes at all!

11

More Dirty Tricks

Nancy turned the steering wheel sharply to the left, and her tires shrieked in protest. Next to her, Cheryl gripped the dashboard and shouted, "Watch out!"

Nancy's convertible cleared the station wagon's rear fender by only a few inches. She worked frantically to pump the brake pedal to build up pressure, but there was no resistance at all.

Quickly, Nancy forced the transmission into low gear, then yanked up on the hand brake. The little car began to slow down but not enough. Looking ahead, Nancy saw with horror that they were fast approaching a busy intersection. She couldn't possibly steer into that steady stream of traffic without someone getting badly hurt.

"Hold on!" Nancy shouted to Cheryl. She steered the car toward the concrete curb on the right, grazing it with her front, then her rear, wheel. The steering wheel vibrated madly, but she gripped it tighter and kept forcing the convertible slightly to the right, just enough to keep the tire in contact with the curb. The tortured rubber squealed loudly and sent up a nauseating smell, but the car gradually slowed to a halt. The front end of the convertible stuck slightly out into the crowded intersection, but cars were able to swerve around it.

"Whew!" exclaimed Cheryl. "That was close!"

"Uh-huh. No brakes," Nancy explained. She unclasped her hands from the steering wheel and wiggled her fingers, which ached from gripping the wheel so tightly.

"What happened?" Cheryl asked.

Nancy released her seat belt and opened her door. "Good question," she said grimly. She got out, knelt down on the pavement, and peered under the Mustang. Something was dripping from near the left front wheel, and she reached and caught a drop on her forefinger. It was a fairly thick pink liquid—hydraulic fluid from the brake line.

She straightened up. "Cheryl," she called, "would you pass me the flashlight from the glove compartment?"

Nancy had to lie down on her side to get a good view under the car, but what she saw confirmed her suspicion. The hydraulic line to the left front wheel had a break in it, just a few inches from the brake itself. The edges of the break were too smooth for it to have occurred naturally. Someone had deliberately nicked the tough plastic tubing with a knife to weaken it, knowing that it would hold for a while, then burst when the brakes were applied strongly. It was only by chance that she and Cheryl hadn't been killed.

As Nancy sat up, a motorcycle roared up and stopped beside her. The rider was unrecognizable behind his dark visor, but a second later he pulled out a camera, then raised his visor to focus on Nancy, Cheryl, and the disabled car.

"Eric!" Nancy cried. "What are you doing here?"

Taking off his helmet, Eric hung it from the handlebars and called back, "Taking pictures, of course. I saw you and Cheryl leaving and decided to follow you."

He got off the motorcycle and walked over to the side of the Mustang as Nancy got to her feet. "You didn't get very far, did you?" he added. "What's wrong?"

"No brakes," Nancy told him. She decided not to say anything about the sabotage yet. Cheryl seemed shaken up enough as it was, and she had to compete soon.

"Wow, you're lucky you weren't hurt! Can I help?"

"Sure, thanks," Nancy said. "Could you find a

pay phone and call the garage for me? I don't think I ought to leave the car." She turned to Cheryl, who was just getting out of the car. "What about you?" she asked. "What do you want to do now?"

"I'm going back to the field," Cheryl replied unsteadily.

"I'll give you a ride on my bike," Eric offered. "It brought me all the way from Washington, so I guess it'll make it back to the school."

She shook her head. "I'd rather walk, thanks."

"What about your lunch?" Nancy asked.

"I'll just have to skip it, I guess," said Cheryl, shrugging.

"Before a race? Are you sure?" Nancy asked. Seeing the puzzled look on Eric's face, she explained about the protein drink.

"Hey, no problem," he said. "After I call the garage, I'll run by your house and pick it up. Will somebody be there?"

"Good idea." Nancy found the number of the garage in the glove compartment and wrote it down. Then she scribbled a note to Hannah.

Eric put on his helmet, started the motorcycle with a roar, and wheeled off down the road.

"Is it okay if I leave you here all alone?" Cheryl asked. "I feel like I need some time to get myself together before I have to warm up for the hundred-meter sprint."

"I understand," Nancy said. "Don't worry about me. I'll just wait until the tow truck comes, then come back to the field. I hope I don't miss your race."

"Don't worry about it if you do," Cheryl replied. "It's only the preliminary." With a wave, she started back toward the athletic field.

Nancy smiled at Cheryl's self-confidence. It didn't even occur to her that she might not make it to the finals. But after all, she knew her own ability, and she probably had a pretty clear idea of the abilities of her opponents as well. If Cheryl was sure that she would make the finals, then she almost certainly would—unless she was sabotaged. It was up to Nancy to make sure that didn't happen.

With a soft toot of its horn, a gleaming red tow truck turned the corner, zipped past, made a quick U-turn, and backed up to the front of Nancy's car. The driver climbed down and said, "Hi, Nancy. What's the trouble? Battery dead?"

"Hi, Frank," Nancy greeted him. "Worse than that, I'm afraid. I've got a broken brake line."

"Really? That doesn't happen much. There was a guy last year whose brake line got chewed up by raccoons, but he lives way out of town. Let's take a look."

He lay down on the pavement and looked under the car. When he sat back up, the smile had vanished from his face. "Nancy, I hate to tell you this—"

"I know. Somebody doesn't like me."

"You said it."

"How hard will it be to fix?" Nancy asked.

"A cinch," Frank assured her. "Just put in a new hose, replace the fluid, and bleed the system." He glanced at his watch. "If my parts man has the right hose in stock, I can have it done this evening."

"Great," she told him.

"Give me a call around four," he added. "I'll know by then."

"Thanks a lot, Frank," Nancy said. She left him hooking up her car to his truck.

Back at the field, she observed that the games were in full swing. The shot-putters were still competing. A group of athletes had collected at one end of the long-jump runway, and at the other end of the field, a pole-vaulter soared into the air and came down, bringing the crossbar down with him. On the track, a girls' relay race was about to start.

Nancy noticed Bess standing near the javelin throw, and she went to join her.

"Where have you been?" Bess demanded. "You missed all the excitement."

Nancy gave Bess a concerned look. "What happened?" she asked. "Was anybody hurt?"

"Hurt? Of course not," Bess said. "Why? You mean there have been more accidents?"

Nancy told her about the near-accident in the Mustang.

"Wow!" Bess exclaimed, giving Nancy a worried look. "You guys are lucky to be alive!"

"I know. And now it's more important than ever for me to get to the bottom of this case," Nancy said. "What was the excitement you mentioned?"

"A guy from South America just tied the world record for the hurdles," Bess told her. Her round face became flushed with excitement. "Isn't that fantastic? A world record, right here in River Heights!"

Nancy chuckled. "You're going to be a devoted sports fan by the time the weekend's over," she teased.

"I can't help it," Bess admitted. "They're really great athletes, and they're so totally wrapped up in what they're doing. It's pretty inspiring. I'm even thinking about starting an exercise program myself," she added, patting her tummy. "I could stand to drop a few pounds."

"Watch out," Nancy said mischievously. "Muscle is denser than fat, you know. The better shape you're in, the more you'll weigh."

"Really? Well, then, I guess I'll have to forget that idea." Bess grinned. "Hey, I have some other news, too. I was talking to that girl Annelise before, and you know what she told me? I said something about Willy and Cheryl, and she said that Willy and *Marta* had a big romance going a while back. Then Helga made Marta break it off because she said it was interfering with Marta's training.''

"So it was Marta who broke up with Willy, was it?" Nancy mused. "I hadn't heard that part of it. I wonder how he took it?"

"I guess now he's too wrapped up in Cheryl to care one way or the other," said Bess.

Nancy thought for a moment. "Yes, but that could be partly an act," she pointed out. "What if he's harassing Marta to get back at her?"

"But then, why all the dirty tricks directed at Cheryl?" Bess protested.

"Maybe as a smoke screen, to keep us from suspecting him—although some of the tricks have been really dangerous. How about this? Willy makes threatening calls to Marta, steals her special honey, and so on. And *Helga*, thinking that Cheryl is behind the harassment, tries to get back at her with these dirty tricks."

"Sure, that works," Bess agreed. "And it explains why all the incidents are so different—because different people are behind them!"

"First call, girls' hundred-meter sprint," a loudspeaker voice boomed.

"That's Cheryl's event," Nancy said. "Come on, let's get over to the starting line. If someone's trying to sabotage Cheryl, this would be a good time to strike."

The competitors in the event were on the grass near the starting line. Some were sitting down, doing last-minute stretches. Others, Marta and Cheryl among them, were simply standing around waiting. Both Eric and Steve were circling around, snapping photos.

"Hello," Annelise called as Nancy and Bess approached. She was standing with her legs apart, bending down and touching the toes of each leg in turn. "You have come to watch us run? It is hard work but great fun."

Cheryl, who was standing nearby, turned around and smiled. She looked looser and more relaxed than she had been after the incident in the Mustang.

"Annelise is right," she said. "Maybe you two should work out with us tomorrow."

Bess backed away, a look of genuine horror on her face, and Cheryl, Annelise, and a couple of other runners laughed.

"Did Eric get back in time with your lunch?" Nancy asked.

"He sure did," replied Cheryl. "He even brought me two cans. One vanilla and one straw-berry."

"What is this?" Annelise asked. "Lunch in a can?"

"Sure, it's protein drink. Here, there's one left. Take a look." Cheryl bent down and looked into her gym bag, then stopped. For one instant she remained there, frozen. Then she straightened up, and with a cry, flung the bag away from her.

12

A Telltale Photo

Nancy and Bess rushed over to Cheryl's side. "What is it?" Nancy asked. "What's wrong?"

"I can't take any more of this!" Cheryl was practically in tears. "Every time I turn around, there's something else!"

The other runners had clustered around and were murmuring to one another. Nancy kneeled down and looked into Cheryl's gym bag. There, on top of a spare set of running gear, was a sheet of paper. The words pasted across the top read, "You just blue your last chance." Underneath was a photo of Cheryl crossing the finish line in a race. A red X had been savagely scratched across her image.

Nancy straightened up. "Did you touch this note yet?" she asked Cheryl.

"Oh, I don't know, I might have," Cheryl

107

replied. "I guess I must have, when I reached in for the can of protein drink, to show Annelise."

"Would you have seen it if it was there before, when you took out the can you drank?"

"What does it matter? All I—" Cheryl paused to rub her eyes and forehead. "I'm sorry, Nancy," she resumed in a distraught voice. "I know you're trying to help. Let me think . . . Wait, now I remember. Eric brought the drinks to me. I took the vanilla and asked him to put the other one away."

"So the last person to handle your gym bag was Eric?" Nancy asked.

"I guess so, but—"

"Cheryl, over here!" Eric called. The circle of spectators parted just enough for him to take a picture. "What's the problem?" he asked, coming over to Cheryl.

"Cheryl just found a threatening note in her bag," Bess explained.

Nancy added, "It wasn't there when you put her protein drink in, was it?"

"I don't think so. Let me see." Before Nancy could warn Eric not to touch the note, he bent down and picked it up.

"Hey," he said, staring. "That's my photo! What's it doing here?"

"What do you mean, your photo?" Nancy asked. She took the note from him, holding it by the corner, though she didn't have much hope of lifting prints from it after the way Eric had handled it.

"It's mine! I took that shot. It was at a meet a couple of months ago. That was the first time I met Cheryl, right?"

"Right." Cheryl nodded. "I remember."

"This looks like it was cut from a magazine," observed Nancy.

"Yeah," said Eric. "It must be from *Der Läufer*. It's a German sports magazine. The name means 'the runner.' That's the only place I sold the photo."

Nancy looked at the reverse side of the picture. "It does look like German," she observed.

"May I look?" Willy inquired from behind Nancy. He looked over her shoulder, bending down to get a clearer view. "Yes," he said. "This is German. It is about a track meet that happened very recently. It must be the latest issue of the magazine. I have not yet seen it."

"*I* have," Cheryl said. She thrust out her arm and pointed at Marta. "She was reading it yesterday!"

Eyes wide, Marta stared at Cheryl. She took a nervous step backward. Helga stepped in front of Marta and glared at Cheryl. "You will leave her alone," she announced. "If you do not, I will do my best to have you disqualified from the games and barred from international competition."

Cheryl's face paled, but she stood her ground.

"Make her show us the magazine," she insisted. "I bet the page with my picture on it is missing."

A look of worry crossed Helga's face. She turned and spoke in a low voice to Marta, who began to look even more nervous.

"You have no right to make demands on us," Helga said, turning back to face Cheryl. "Even if a page is gone from a magazine, it proves nothing at all."

"Then it *is* gone!" Cheryl exclaimed. "I knew it!"

"What's going on here?" The starter pushed his way into the circle of runners. "Didn't any of you hear the last call?"

Nancy stepped over to him and said softly, "I think this race should be postponed a few minutes."

"What? Who are you?"

Nancy showed him the note Mr. Hornby had written on his card.

"Well," he said slowly, "you'll have to speak to the referee. He's the only one who can make a decision like that." He looked around, raised his arm over his head, and waved it in a circle. "He'll be right over."

A barrel-chested man with gray hair strode up a few moments later and said, "What's the hold-up, Fred?"

"This young lady would like the girls' hundred

meter delayed," the starter said, indicating Nancy with his thumb.

Nancy again produced Mr. Hornby's card, explaining that two of the runners had just been put under unusual pressure, and that it wouldn't be fair to run the race before they had time to recover.

The referee thought for a minute or so, tugging at one earlobe, then nodded. "Five minutes, no more," he said. "Fred, you tell the contestants. I'll pass the word to the announcer."

"A delay?" Cheryl asked. "Because of me? Well, don't bother. I'm pulling out!"

Nancy looked at her in surprise.

"Wait," Willy called to the starter. He put his arm around Cheryl's shoulders. "Do not listen to her. She is very upset and does not know what she is saying."

"Yes, I do!" shouted Cheryl. She pulled away from Willy. "I'm saying I've had it! I don't know why Marta hates me so much, but if she wants to win this badly, let her. I hope the medal chokes her! Everyone will know that she won it dishonestly."

"You came a long way to run in this race," Willy pointed out. "You will make yourself very sad if you do not do it."

"Yeah, and I could wind up very dead unless I get away from this place," said Cheryl. "You don't believe me? Ask Nancy what happened to us just an hour ago!"

Eric came forward and said, "Cheryl, you're not going to let yourself be intimidated, are you? What about your sports career? What about our project?"

"It's your project, not mine," Cheryl reminded him. "And I couldn't care less about it."

"Well, you should care," said Eric. "You've got the ability to be a star. A couple of solid wins, my photos in *Athletics Weekly,* some news stories about how you triumphed over a campaign of threats and dirty tricks—*everyone* will know your name!"

Willy stepped between Eric and Cheryl. "This is enough," he said. "If she is to run, Cheryl must have time to find her center. We shall leave her alone now, and she will prepare herself, yes?"

"She can speak for herself," Eric said, raising his voice. "All I want is for her to stay in the race and win."

Willy put his hand on Eric's shoulder. "I tell you, you are bothering her," he said, giving Eric a little push.

Eric pushed back. "Keep your hands to yourself, buddy," he said, sticking out his chin.

"Will you two stop it?" pleaded Cheryl. "Just let me alone, both of you!"

Before either of the guys could react, the starter came over. "Everyone except the runners in the girls' hundred-meter sprint please clear the area . . . at once," he instructed in a forceful voice.

Willy and Eric glared at each other for a few seconds more, then turned and walked toward the sidelines.

Nancy had watched their angry exchange closely, but neither young man had revealed anything except that tempers had quickly heated up. Catching Cheryl's gaze, she raised a questioning eyebrow.

Cheryl took a deep breath, let it out, and said, "Oh, I guess I'll run. That's what I came here for, after all. And anyone who tries any tricks on me is going to be very sorry!"

A whistle blast from the finish-line judge gave the "all ready." Nancy and Bess watched the runners remove their warm-up clothes and take their positions at the starting line.

"Come on," Nancy said. "If we hurry, we might catch the finish."

As they walked up the track, Bess said, "There's something weird about that note in Cheryl's bag. Spooky, I guess I mean."

Nancy glanced over at her friend. "You mean the way the word *b-l-u-e* was used instead of *b-l-e-w?* My guess is that it was just a matter of which word was easier to find in a magazine headline."

"That makes sense," said Bess. "But why put

that picture of Cheryl on the note? I mean, it had to come from that German magazine, right? Why give away a big clue like that?"

Nancy frowned. "And the most recent issue of the magazine, too. It probably hasn't reached any American newsstands yet. That means our note writer is almost certainly a European athlete who knows German well enough to read sports magazines in that language *and* who just arrived from Europe, bringing the magazine along."

"In other words, Marta, who, according to Cheryl, was reading that same magazine just yesterday," Bess said.

"I don't know," Nancy said slowly. "It's almost *too* obvious, like a frame-up. But who's behind it?"

"Beats me," Bess said.

"Unless it was Eric," Nancy said, thinking out loud. "He's the most likely person on this side of the Atlantic to have a copy of that issue of the magazine. And he seems to turn up every time another dirty trick is played on Cheryl."

At that moment the sound of a gunshot interrupted the two girls. They turned around to see the eight runners in the hundred-meter sprint come tearing down the track toward them. The runners' cleats scarcely seemed to touch the track, and the athletes were so evenly matched that Nancy couldn't tell who was leading.

As they whizzed past Nancy and Bess, Nancy

saw that Marta had a small lead, but that Cheryl, the cords of her neck standing out like ropes, was starting to draw even. Annelise, a pace behind them, was holding on to third place.

Bess grabbed Nancy's arm and jumped up and down in excitement. Then, abruptly, the race was over. The pack of runners breasted the ribbon, coasted to a stop, and walked tiredly back to the finish line. Nancy hadn't been able to tell who the winner was, and apparently the judges were having trouble deciding, too. The judges' assistants and the timers huddled together for what seemed like forever.

Finally, the head finish-line judge shook her head and walked across to a field telephone to call the results up to the announcer's booth.

13

A Secret Source

Cheryl, Marta, Annelise, and the other runners stared expectantly up at the loudspeaker as it crackled to life.

"Ladies and gentlemen, here are the results of the girls' hundred-meter sprint. First place, Cheryl Pierce of Washington, D.C., with a time of 10.74 seconds. Second place, Marta Schmidt of Leipzig, Germany . . ."

Cheryl let out a yelp of joy, danced a few steps in place, and reached out to give Willy a hug.

"Well done," Willy said, grinning. "Aren't you happy now that you decided to run?"

"You bet I am!" Noticing Nancy and Bess at the sidelines, Cheryl beckoned them over. Just before they reached Cheryl, Marta approached.

"Congratulations," the German girl said. "You

ran very well." She offered her hand, a little stiffly, and Cheryl took it, just as stiffly.

"Thank you," she said. "You ran very well, too."

Then Marta walked over to where Helga was waiting with her warm-up jacket.

Cheryl accepted handshakes from Nancy, Bess, and the other runners, then started walking back to the starting line to collect her belongings. Nancy was about to follow when she heard raised voices from the sidelines.

"You shoved me on purpose," Eric was saying. "You ruined my shot of the finish!"

"Ha!" Steve replied. "You stepped in front of me. What do you expect me to do, take pictures of your back? And anyway, you don't need help from anyone else to ruin your shots. You can take care of that all by yourself."

Fists clenched, Eric took a step in Steve's direction. "Yeah?" he said. "You'll change your tune after I win the *Athletics Weekly* contest."

"When pigs fly," Steve retorted. He put a protective arm in front of his two cameras but did not retreat.

"Hey, you fellows," the finish-line judge called. "Stop fighting and clear the area. Any more problems from you and I'll have your press passes lifted."

"Yes, ma'am," Eric muttered. Giving Steve a

parting scowl, he stalked off toward the starting line.

"Boy, is Eric in a bad mood," Bess said. "That's two fights he's nearly gotten into in less than ten minutes. Maybe he *is* behind the dirty tricks."

"I'm not convinced of it," Nancy replied slowly. "But it's a possibility I can't just push aside. Hey, there's George," she added, and waved.

"That was some finish, huh?" George said as she came over to them. "You must have been glad to see Cheryl win."

"Sure," said Bess. "But do you know what happened before the start? Cheryl almost pulled out of the race."

"She did? Why?"

"Another note," Nancy said. She told George about someone cutting her brake line and about the threatening words and slashed-over photo. "The odd thing," she concluded, "is that the picture came from a German sports magazine called *Der Läufer.*"

"Really?" George looked at Nancy with narrowed eyes. "I've seen a copy of that. It was in Marta's wastebasket this morning. I pulled it out and saved it because I thought it might be interesting."

"Do you still have it?" Nancy asked excitedly. George nodded.

"Can you run home and get it?" Nancy continued. "If it's the right issue, take a look to see if page— Hold on a sec." She retrieved the threatening message from her pocket and checked the page with the photo of Cheryl. "See if page twenty-three is missing."

"Can it wait until the games finish for the day?" George asked.

Remembering the way her brake pedal had felt as it sank to the floor, Nancy said, "It could be a matter of life and death."

"I'll go right away," George said.

"Thanks, George," Nancy said. "Come back as soon as you can. I'll be around here somewhere. Oh—and while you're home, check for a European magazine in English, with words cut out of the pages."

As George rushed off, Bess took Nancy's arm and pulled her back from the edge of the track. The men's relay races were being announced.

"Oh, look, there's Ramsay," Bess said, pointing over Nancy's shoulder. "I must have missed the second round of the shot put. I wonder how he did. I'll be right back."

Looking over, Nancy saw that the Canadian athlete was talking to Barbara, who waved when she noticed Nancy and Bess. A few moments later, she was at Nancy's side.

"I've got some information for you," Barbara said in a low voice. "Will you walk me over to the press booth?"

The press booth was a roped-off enclosure

equipped with tables and chairs at the far end of the grandstand. When they reached it, Barbara pulled a couple of folding chairs into the corner and sat down.

"I feel like I've been on my feet for two solid days!" she exclaimed. "Anyway, here's the thing. I've been interviewing as many of the athletes as I can. They're all starting to get edgy about this meet. Most of them don't know exactly what's been going on, but they sense that *something* is, and they don't like it a bit."

"I'm not surprised," said Nancy. "That's one of the reasons I want to get to the bottom of this case as quickly as possible."

Barbara nodded. "Well, maybe this will help. I met this sportswriter today, a very experienced guy who's covered events all over the world. And while we were talking, Helga Roth walked by. He was very surprised to see her here. According to him, during the last Summer Olympics, she was accused of pulling a series of dirty tricks against members of another team. Nothing was ever proven, apparently, but a lot of people believed that there must have been something to the accusation."

"You mean they figured, Where there's smoke there's fire?"

Barbara nodded again. "Something like that. It's not what you'd call strong evidence, but—"

"Every bit helps," Nancy said. "Do you think I could talk to your reporter friend myself and get more details?"

"There's no point," Barbara said. "He told me everything he remembered, which wasn't any more than I just told you. Oops," she added, looking over Nancy's shoulder. "There's somebody I have to talk to. Sorry to rush off, but I'll see you later."

She stood up and walked quickly away before Nancy could ask her anything more. Nancy leaned back in her chair, frowning. Why was Barbara so reluctant to let Nancy talk to the sportswriter for herself? Was it just a matter of keeping her sources private? Or was it possible that Barbara had made up the whole story?

Nancy shook her head and started walking back to the field. There were at least half a dozen people who'd been behaving suspiciously during the past two days. What she needed was evidence. Proof. *Someone* must have seen the guilty person putting the threatening note in Cheryl's bag or throwing the light switches at the swimming pool—or sabotaging the brakes on Nancy's car. And she had to find that someone before something else happened.

When Nancy arrived at the field, she found Bess still talking to Ramsay Roberts. She walked over to them.

"Hi, Nancy," Bess called. "Isn't it great? Ramsay made it into the finals in both the discus and the shot put!"

"Congratulations," Nancy said. "You're going to have a busy day tomorrow, aren't you?"

"It looks that way," Ramsay said with a grin.

"And not only that," Bess continued, "Ramsay can come to dinner with us tonight."

"With whom?" asked Nancy, puzzled.

"With all of us. You mean you don't know about it yet? Your dad, my parents, and George's parents decided to treat us all to dinner at Le Saint-Tropez."

"Great," Nancy said. Le Saint-Tropez was one of the fanciest restaurants in River Heights.

"It's turning into quite a party," Bess went on. "When I saw Cheryl just now and told her about it, she asked if Willy could come. And then Willy was worried that Annelise would feel left out unless we asked her, too. And, of course, now Ramsay is coming. I bet we'll have a terrific time."

Nancy didn't want to think about what it would be like to have Cheryl, Marta, and Helga at the same dinner table. "It should be a very interesting evening" was all she said.

Bess didn't seem to notice the irony in her voice. "I need to find Marie-Laure," she said. "We'll see you later."

As Bess and Ramsay walked away, the tall

Canadian put his hand on Bess's shoulder and Bess gazed up at him. Nancy shook her head. Cheryl was certainly right about how fast romances developed at these meets!

Nancy looked at her watch. It was getting late. She and Cheryl should probably return home soon. Scanning the field, she started in the direction of the gym.

"Nancy!" someone called. "Over here!"

George was standing on the steps at the end of the grandstand, waving.

"Have you heard about this dinner tonight?" George asked when Nancy reached her.

"Bess was just telling me."

"I was really surprised that everybody agreed. I mean, tomorrow's the final day of the games. I would have thought they'd want to have a simple training meal and get to bed early instead of having dinner at a fancy French restaurant."

Nancy shrugged. "I guess they're all old enough to make up their own minds. Now, stop worrying about dinner and let's get on with our investigation. Did you find that magazine?"

George nodded. "It was right where I'd left it. I didn't see any English-language magazines, though, with or without cut pages."

"But you found *Der Läufer?*" Nancy prompted.

"You bet. And the page you asked about, page twenty-three, was missing. It had been ripped out."

14

Thief in the Night

"The missing page proves it, doesn't it?" said George. "Either Marta or Helga must have made that threatening note and slipped it into Cheryl's bag."

"It looks that way," Nancy replied, "although we'll have to match the page and the magazine to be sure. Do you have the magazine with you?"

"No, I left it at home, hidden in my room. I thought it would be safer there."

"Good idea. It's important evidence." Nancy brushed her reddish blond hair back from her face and tucked it behind one ear. "If Marta or Helga *is* responsible for the sabotage, it's going to take more than just hunches and accusations to stop them. We'll need proof. Be sure to bring the magazine to the meet with you tomorrow morning, okay? I hope that by then we'll be in a position to wrap this up."

Nancy glanced at her watch. "I'd better be getting home. Oops—I just remembered. My car is still at the garage. Can you give Cheryl and me a lift?"

"Sure," George said. "Come on, let's go."

"You know," Nancy added as they walked toward the gym to find Cheryl, "I can't help feeling bad about this whole thing. It's funny—I was really looking forward to the games. After all, how often does anyone get the chance to meet world-class athletes and watch them in action? But now I'm starting to wish I'd never heard of them."

A flash went off a few feet from Nancy's face just as she was lifting a slice of steak with white pepper sauce from her plate. She frowned as a dollop of sauce fell off the fork and smeared itself on the leg of her new black slacks.

Willy, who was sitting on Nancy's left, dipped his napkin in his ice water and offered it to her.

"No, thanks," she said. She was starting to blot the sauce with her own napkin when another flash went off.

"Is this usual in the U.S., to have people take photographs as you eat?" Willy asked.

Nancy looked around. The dinner party had

grown so big that the maître d' had put them in a small private dining room. The Faynes and their guests, Marta and Helga, were seated at one end of the long table. Steve seemed to be spending most of his time in that part of the room, and Nancy couldn't help wondering if Barbara had tipped him off that Helga and Marta might be getting some unusual publicity in the next day or two.

Eric continued to hover around Cheryl, who was sitting across the table from Willy, next to Carson Drew, Nancy's father.

"No, this isn't usual," Nancy said, replying to Willy's question. "As a matter of fact, I'm not sure what Eric and Steve are doing here at all. I don't think anybody invited them."

She hadn't meant for Eric to overhear her, but her words must have carried farther than she had intended them to. Eric grinned at her, and said "We're just covering the games, Nancy."

Making her an exaggerated bow, he stepped to one side to get a better angle on Cheryl smiling at Carson Drew.

"He goes too far," Willy muttered. "Cheryl should never have said she would allow this project. He is only using her for his own purposes. The medals she wins and the times she turns in are the only publicity she needs."

"It must be nice to see a photo of yourself crossing the finish line, though," Nancy commented. "And to know that lots of other people saw it, too."

Willy shrugged. "Nice, perhaps," he said. "But the experience itself and the knowledge of what you have done—that should be enough."

Still, camera lights continued to flash for the remainder of the evening. When the dessert arrived, everyone began to clap. George's mother had ordered a big oval cake decorated to look like an athletic field, complete with running track, a pole-vaulting setup, and even an array of tiny hurdles.

Carson Drew stood up. "No long speeches," he said. "I promise. But I can't let the evening end without saying how happy all of us in River Heights are that you remarkable young people have come here to share your talents and dedication with us. Thank you."

When the applause died down, Willy glanced around the table at his fellow athletes, then stood up in turn. "It is for us to thank you," he said, "for taking us into your homes, for giving us a chance to try ourselves against one another, for allowing us to see something of your wonderful country, and most important"—he paused and looked across the table at Cheryl—"to give us the chance to make wonderful new friends. We will not forget our visit here."

As everyone clapped and cheered, Eric and Steve were jockeying for the best camera angles.

"Okay, buddy," Steve said. "You've been on my case for two days now, and I've had enough!"

Eric whirled and said, "Yeah? Too bad you can't use a camera as well as you use your mouth!"

Carson stood up again and said, "May I remind you gentlemen that this is a private party? It might be better if you were to leave now—and quietly."

Steve and Eric looked at each other, then glanced around the room at the disapproving faces of the others. After an awkward pause, they each muttered, "Sorry," and headed for the door.

Mrs. Fayne cut the cake and started passing slices around, but the fight between Eric and Steve had taken some of the fun out of the dinner. As soon as everyone had finished the cake, George said, "I think we ought to break up early. These guys have a meet tomorrow, after all."

Steve and Eric were waiting for them outside the restaurant door, and Nancy was glad to see her father give them a friendly smile. He had been right to ask them to leave, but there was no point in starting a feud. There was already enough fighting going on in this group!

"Willy?" Nancy said when they reached the parking lot. "Can we give you a ride?"

"Thank you," he said, taking Cheryl's hand.

"Marta, Helga?" George called. The Faynes

had parked next to Nancy's father. "You can come in back with me."

"Ramsay and Annelise are coming with us," Bess announced. "And Marie-Laure, of course."

Nancy realized with a guilty start that she had barely said more than a hello to the young French girl all evening. She was about to go over to her when Mr. Fayne exclaimed, "Oh, no, not again! The car won't start."

He climbed out with a flashlight in his hand and raised the hood. Nancy went over and peered down at the engine. "Do you know what the problem is?" she asked.

"Not really," he grumbled. "It must be something electrical, but no one has been able to track it down. Usually it just seems to fix itself."

"Mr. Fayne?" said Willy. "Would you mind to let me look at it? I know something about automobiles."

"I'd be grateful," Mr. Fayne said.

Willy took the flashlight from Mr. Fayne and he began to pull and push at the tangle of wires.

Nancy watched curiously. Willy certainly seemed to know his way around cars. Could he have been the one who had sabotaged her Mustang? Eric and Annelise had also gathered around. Nancy heard Annelise give Willy some suggestions about what might be wrong. She was about to join them when Bess came over with Marie-Laure. As Nancy chatted with them, she

129

kept glancing at the group bent under the Faynes' hood but didn't have a chance to watch closely.

"Try the engine now," Willy suggested after a few minutes.

Mr. Fayne got in and turned the key. The engine caught at once.

Willy was just closing the hood of the car when suddenly Eric said in alarm, "My bag! Where's my camera bag?"

Nancy hurried over to him. "Where did you leave it?"

"On the ground, next to my motorcycle." He was looking frantically from side to side. "I put it down when you guys came out of the restaurant, and now it's gone. All my equipment is in it—everything!"

"Don't worry," Nancy said. "No one's been in the parking lot except us. It's bound to be around here somewhere." Unless someone in the group took it on purpose, Nancy added to herself. She looked quickly toward Helga and Marta, who were standing quietly at the side of the Faynes' car. "We'll all help you look," she told Eric.

Nancy borrowed Mr. Fayne's flashlight and bent down to look underneath the nearest cars. All she found were a couple of discarded soda cans. Straightening up again, she headed toward the dark shadows of the surrounding shrubbery.

"Here," Annelise's voice called from beyond one of the nearby cars. "Is this it?"

She appeared with a canvas-and-leather bag in her hands, and Eric ran over to her. "Hey, I really don't know how to thank you," he said.

"It was nothing," she replied, handing him the bag.

"Where did you find it?" asked Nancy.

Annelise pointed. "It was under one of those bushes, but the strap was still in sight. That is what led me to it."

"I don't think it got there by accident," Nancy said. "Eric, you'd better check—"

"Oh, no!" he wailed, staring down into the open bag. "My film. It's gone!"

"Don't worry," Carson Drew said. "You can buy more first thing in the morning, before the games begin."

"You don't understand," Eric said, his voice shrill. "This was exposed film. I was planning to mail it to the processors tomorrow."

"You mean—" Nancy began.

"I'm finished." Eric pounded his fist against his forehead. "Wiped out! Every color shot I've taken in the last two days is gone!"

15

Race for the Gold

"Are you sure, Eric?" Nancy asked. "Could you have left the film at home and then forgotten about it?"

"I'm sure, all right," he replied. "It was in there fifteen minutes ago when I changed lenses, and it's not there now. And I know who to blame, too."

Pushing past Nancy and her father, he strode over to Steve, who was standing talking to Marta and George. He grabbed Steve by the shoulder and spun him around.

"Where is it, you dirty thief?" Eric demanded. "What did you do with my film?"

"Get your hands off me!" Steve scoffed, pushing Eric away. "I never touched your film!"

"You knew you couldn't win the contest fair and square, right?" Eric continued, his fists clenched. "So you cheated and stole instead. I ought to flatten your nose!"

"Eric," Nancy said calmly, taking his elbow. "Getting into a fight isn't going to help you find the missing pictures."

Willy had stepped in between the two photographers and was talking in a low voice to Steve, who said, "You think I'm going to let him call me names like that?"

Willy kept talking, and finally Steve said, "Okay, okay!" He took a step forward and said, "Listen, Eric, I didn't steal your film, and I'm sorry it's gone." He took his camera bag and opened it so Eric could see its contents. "Here. Take a look if you don't believe me."

Nancy handed Eric the flashlight. He looked in the bag, but his film wasn't there. "If I was wrong in saying you did it, I'm sorry," he said grudgingly. "But I'm warning you, I still mean to win the *Athletics Weekly* contest. I have all my black-and-white shots in a safe place, and some of them would knock your socks off!"

The tension had eased, and once again everyone began to get ready to leave.

Nancy went over to Eric and took him aside. "What exactly was on those rolls?" she asked.

"I told you, all the color shots I've taken since arriving in River Heights."

Nancy thought quickly. That meant the rolls he'd shot during the ceremony at City Hall were

133

gone—including any pictures of someone pushing Cheryl off the stands. "Would the missing pictures include Cheryl winning the hundred-meter sprint today?" she asked. "Could you have gotten a picture of someone doing something they shouldn't?"

Eric shook his head. "No. I'm planning to shoot tomorrow's final with high-speed color film, but today I used black-and-white."

"What about this morning, at the swimming pool? I remember you were using two cameras. Was one of them loaded with color?"

"Sure," he replied.

"Did you take any pictures just before the lights went out? Is there any chance you got a shot of the person who turned them off? That would be solid proof of who's been harassing Cheryl."

Eric thought for a moment, then shook his head. "Nope," he said. "No way. I remember I was focusing on Cheryl, hoping to get her in middive. I had my back to the entrance at that point."

"Oh, well." Nancy sighed. "It was an idea, anyway."

"Maybe this is just more harassment," Eric said. "Maybe somebody simply doesn't want Cheryl to have the kind of publicity she'd get if I win the contest."

"Nancy?" Carson Drew called from the car. "We have to go."

"Right, Dad," she replied. "Okay, Eric, thanks. And don't worry too much. I have a feeling that you'll get your film back."

"I hope so," he said in a gloomy voice. "There are a lot of shots I'd hate to lose. See you tomorrow."

A few minutes later, Nancy waved goodbye and then got into her father's car. Carson Drew pulled up in front of the house where Willy was staying.

"I'll get out here, too," Cheryl said, "and walk back later."

"Are you sure you know the way?" Mr. Drew asked.

"I still have my map," she replied. "Don't worry, I won't be very long. Remember, I'm in training."

"All right," Nancy's father said. "But be careful walking home. We'll leave the front door open. Be sure to lock it after you come in."

After she and her father returned home, Nancy sat down at the desk in her room and made up a chart. Down the left margin she wrote the names of all the people who had any connection with the case: Helga, Marta, Cheryl, Barbara, Steve, Eric, Ramsay, Willy, and Annelise.

Across the top she listed all the important incidents, beginning with Cheryl's near-fall from the stands during the welcoming ceremony at

City Hall and ending with the theft of Eric's undeveloped film.

Next Nancy began to fill in the boxes on the chart. For each incident, all of the people got a check if they could have been responsible for it, an X if they couldn't have, or a question mark if she wasn't sure. She had planned to circle the boxes where she didn't know what to put, but to her surprise, there weren't any. She knew more about everyone's whereabouts and actions than she had realized.

Once she completed the chart, she sat back and examined it closely. Whom could she eliminate? Ramsay, certainly; he hadn't been anywhere nearby during some of the major incidents. What about Steve? He had several check marks. For that matter, Cheryl, Marta, Helga, Eric, Barbara, Willy, and Annelise all had some X's, too.

Nancy tossed her ballpoint down on the desk in disgust. The only thing the chart proved was that there were plenty of suspects! To make matters worse, if more than one person was involved—if, for instance, Cheryl was harassing Marta and Helga was harassing Cheryl—then no one person could be eliminated just because he or she couldn't have committed *all* the tricks. She hoped the magazine George had would provide some concrete proof, but she wouldn't know that until the next morning.

A yawn that felt as if it would crack her jaw reminded Nancy that she had been up and active since daybreak. After taking another long look at the chart, she put it away and started getting ready for bed.

The following morning, the weather was perfect—sunny and clear, with just enough of a breeze to keep it from being too warm. For a moment, Nancy turned her face up toward the sun, eyes closed. Then a burst of applause from the stands called her back to reality. A hurdles race had just ended. Even before the results were announced, a dozen uniformed aides scurried onto the track to remove the hurdles and prepare the track for the next event.

"Oh, there you are," Barbara said, coming up to Nancy. "I was looking for you. I hear from Steve that I missed a pretty exciting evening last night."

"I guess you could say that," Nancy replied. "How are you doing?"

"My interviews are going pretty well but the reason I was looking for you . . ." She paused to clear her throat, looking embarrassed. "You know that story I passed along to you yesterday?"

"About Helga and the Olympics, you mean?" Nancy leaned forward.

"Uh-huh. I thought it was a terrific story, especially the way it tied in to what's been going on here. So I've been going around talking to people, trying to dig up more material." She fell silent.

"And?" Nancy prodded.

"And it looks like it's just a lot of nasty gossip," Barbara admitted. "The guy who told me about the accusations—the sportswriter? He seems to have a long-standing grudge against Helga. I couldn't find out why."

"But what about the accusations themselves?" asked Nancy.

"The word is that they were made by a runner whose father is a very important politician in her home country. Apparently, she's not much of an athlete, but the others on her team, including the coach, were very eager to find excuses for her poor showing. The accusation against Helga was one of the things they came up with."

"I see," Nancy said, disappointed. That meant the case was just as open-ended as ever. Excusing herself, Nancy set off across the field to look for George. She must have arrived by now with the magazine, but Nancy hadn't seen her yet.

She turned in surprise as a hand touched her arm. "Just the person I'm looking for," Nancy said, smiling.

"I just got here," George explained. "I stayed home until after Helga and Marta left. I didn't want to take the chance of them seeing me with their magazine."

"Do you have it with you?" Nancy asked.

George patted her oversize shoulder bag. "Right here." George reached into her bag, pulled out the magazine, and handed it to Nancy. On the cover was a dynamic color photo of four men charging down a track, knees high and arms pumping like mad. Across the top, in big red letters, were the words *Der Läufer*.

Nancy thumbed through to page twenty-three. Just as George had said, the page had been torn out, so roughly and hastily that a large corner of the photo of Cheryl still clung to the center of the magazine.

Nancy stared at it. "But——" she began. Then she thrust the magazine back into George's hands, opened her own shoulder bag, and found the brown envelope that contained the previous day's threatening notes. "Look at this," she told George.

"It's the same, all right," George said, "I guess that proves it."

"If it proves anything, it proves that Helga and Marta are innocent," Nancy proclaimed. "This photo was neatly cut from the magazine with a pair of scissors, not torn out. And this corner of the picture is still inside Marta's copy."

George stared at Nancy. "Then who——"

"Someone else who had a copy of the magazine," Nancy cut in. "Someone like Eric, who got a copy because his photo was in it. Or any of the

German-speaking runners could have brought a copy."

"And anyone else might have stolen it from them," George pointed out, "if they wanted a picture of Cheryl and knew one was in it."

Nancy pounded her thigh with her fist. "Every time I think I'm starting to get somewhere with this case, the evidence turns out to point fourteen different ways instead of one! And the awful part is, I'm sure I'm forgetting or overlooking something crucial. It's right here"—she tapped her temple—"but I just don't know what it is."

"It'll come to you, Nancy," George remarked. "It always does."

"Hey, listen!" Nancy said excitedly. "The announcer is calling the finals of the girls' hundred-meter sprint. That's Cheryl's and Marta's big race. Come on!"

Nancy hurried across the field toward the starting line, with George close behind her. The finalists were already starting to take off their warm-up suits. After the uniform white suits, it was almost a shock to see jerseys and shorts in a rainbow of colors.

Nancy stopped so suddenly that George bumped into her. "Pink," Nancy muttered to herself, looking at Cheryl's pink running shorts. "Pink . . . and white. Of course! I'm an idiot!"

George looked at her as if she were crazy, but Nancy paid no attention. Looking quickly toward the track, Nancy saw that the runners were moving toward the starting blocks. Even from twenty feet away, Nancy could sense the tension between Cheryl and Marta.

"Come on!" Nancy cried, dragging George by the arm. "Let's get down to the finish line before it's too late!"

They raced toward the little crowd of officials and spectators, but before Nancy could ask the head finish-line judge to postpone the race, he blew his whistle. A split second later, the starter's pistol went off with a bang.

Nancy let out a cry of dismay. "George, I have a feeling something terrible is about to happen, and there's nothing we can do to stop it!"

16

Winners and Losers

The pack of girls dashed up the track toward the finish line. Soon they were close enough for Nancy and George to recognize faces. Cheryl and Marta were so evenly matched that it was impossible to tell which one was ahead. The crowd in the stands was on its feet and cheering wildly.

Suddenly, Nancy thought she saw Marta and Cheryl glance at each other instead of staying focused on the finish line. Apparently their concentration broke for a split second, and with it, their stride.

"Oh, no!" George wailed.

She and Nancy watched in amazement as the runner in third place surged into the lead. Two ticks of the clock later, and she was raising her arms to breast the tape.

Annelise had won the gold medal!

Marta and Cheryl were only inches behind her, still so evenly matched that Nancy had no idea which of them had reached the line first. Nancy had to speak loudly to be heard over the applause of the crowd. "I'll be right back," she told George.

Nancy hurried toward the gym. She wanted to be sure to get to the locker room before the runners did. As she made her way across the field, she heard the announcer give the results of the race. The winner, of course, was Annelise Dumont, of Basel, Switzerland. Nancy noted that Annelise's time was a few hundredths of a second slower than Cheryl's time of the day before. That was surprising since in finals athletes usually turned in better times than in preliminary heats.

When Nancy entered the locker room, it was empty. She paused for a moment, trying to recall the location of the locker she was looking for. About halfway down the left side of the aisle, but which? The corner of one of the doors was slightly dented, and the paint was scratched. That was it! She rummaged quickly through her shoulder bag, found her lock-picking tools, and set to work on the locker door.

Just as the lock snapped open, she heard footsteps in the corridor. Glancing briefly over her shoulder, she tugged the locker door open.

Right in front of her, in a heap at the bottom of the locker, was the proof she was looking for!

She picked it up, gave it a quick inspection, shoved it into her shoulder bag, then slammed the locker closed. She hurried out of the locker room just as a woman wearing a security-guard uniform was coming in. The guard looked closely at Nancy but didn't stop her or ask any questions.

Nancy raced back to the track. Lionel Hornby was standing near the finish line, and the dismayed look on his face told Nancy that things weren't going smoothly.

Cheryl and Helga were arguing hotly with each other and with the finish judges and referee. Eric and Steve were taking picture after picture, and Barbara's pen raced across her pad. Willy was talking softly to George and Bess, while Marta stood by silently, a look of misery on her face. Annelise, alone, was hovering nearby as well. Her face looked almost as unhappy as Marta's.

Mr. Hornby looked up as Nancy approached. He must have seen the look of triumph on her face, because a flash of hope appeared in his eyes.

"Nancy," he said. "You have something?"

"A solution, I think," she replied. She talked to him for a few moments. A frown came over his face as he listened. At last he nodded and said, "I guess we don't have any choice, do we?"

"I'm afraid not," Nancy told him.

"Then let's get it over with." He stepped over to Helga and Cheryl and said, "I think Nancy Drew has a way to resolve your disagreements. Nancy?"

The other athletes and officials drew closer.

"Since the first day of the games," Nancy began, "two of the athletes have been the victims of threats and harassment—Cheryl Pierce and Marta Schmidt. For lots of reasons, each of them suspected the other. And when Mr. Hornby asked me to investigate, that was my first thought, too—that each of them was harassing the other."

"Nancy!" Cheryl exclaimed. "And I thought you believed me!"

"I did," Nancy replied with an apologetic glance. "But only later. There were some other suspects, too, such as Ramsay or Willy or Helga, who might have had reasons to get back at either Cheryl or Marta. Not to mention the possibility that some of the incidents were a smoke screen to hide the real motive."

"Nancy," Mr. Hornby interrupted, "we have to resolve this quickly. We're holding up the games."

"Okay," Nancy replied. She looked around and caught Eric's eye. "Last night, somebody stole all of Eric's undeveloped color film. Why? To keep Cheryl from winning the public notice

145

his pictures of her might bring?" Nancy shook her head. "More likely, that film was somehow dangerous to the thief.

"During the opening ceremonies, Cheryl felt someone trying to push her off the stands," Nancy went on. "She could have been really hurt. And Eric was taking color photos at that moment, using a telephoto lens. The person who shoved Cheryl couldn't have known that at the time, but if he or she found out later, the person would have realized that the photographs could be incriminating." She turned to the photographer. "Eric? Did you talk to anyone about those photos?"

Eric reddened as everyone turned to look at him. "Well, sure I did," he admitted. "You remember. You asked me about them the other day, at your house."

"Do you remember who else was there?"

"Cheryl, of course, and you," he replied. "And weren't Ramsay and Annelise there too?"

"Now, wait a second," Ramsay began. "Are you trying—"

Nancy held up her hand. "Let me go on," she said. "Yesterday Cheryl received a threatening note that included a mutilated photo of her that had appeared in a German runners' magazine."

Nancy pulled the copy of *Der Läufer* from her bag. "Marta?" she said. "Is this yours?"

"I have such a magazine," the girl stammered. "But how . . . why . . . ?"

"Marta! Say nothing at all!" Helga interrupted loudly. "She is trying to trap you!"

"The photo of Cheryl was on page twenty-three," Nancy continued, opening the magazine. "You can see that it's been torn out."

Marta's eyes filled with tears. "Yes, I did that," she confessed. "I was very sad, very upset. When I saw that picture, I couldn't stand it. I tore it out and crumpled it and threw it away. Afterward I was ashamed that I had been so childish. But I did not send any threats to Cheryl."

"I know you didn't," said Nancy. "The photo on the threatening note had been neatly cut from the magazine—from somebody else's copy of it."

"*I* have a copy of it," Eric said. "But it's back in Washington, and it still has all its pages. Especially the one with Cheryl's photo."

"I didn't think you'd damage one of your own pictures like that, anyway," Nancy remarked. "Even just a copy. No, the threatening note convinced me that we were probably looking for someone, a runner, who speaks German and would read the magazine regularly."

"There are not many Germans here," Helga said. "And even fewer who are runners. Do you mean to accuse me? I warn you, I have dealt with false accusations before now."

"I didn't say someone who *is* German," Nancy told her. "I said someone who *speaks* German."

Willy looked up from comforting Cheryl. "Of course I speak German," he said. "In my part of Switzerland everyone does. That is not proof of anything."

"Maybe not proof, but it does point to somebody. Somebody who speaks German, who knew that Eric might have a damaging photo of the welcoming ceremony, and above all, who profited most from Cheryl's and Marta's frazzled nerves. Profited to the extent of winning a gold medal."

Nancy turned and stared accusingly at Annelise.

Annelise stared back at her defiantly, but her face went pale, and she seemed hardly to breathe. "This is false. You and your friend Cheryl wish to steal my victory today, that is all. You have no proof at all."

Nancy tightened her lips. As she reached into her shoulder bag, she said, "I'm afraid I do have proof." She pulled out a pair of warm-up pants and unfolded them to show a series of blotchy pink stains.

"That is nothing but some stains from juice," Annelise proclaimed. "It has nothing to do with anything."

Nancy shook her head. "Annelise, you know as well as I do that these stains were made by the hydraulic fluid that spilled on you when you

148

tampered with the brakes of my car. Any police lab will be able to show that."

Annelise took in a sharp breath but said nothing.

"And your interest in fixing Mr. Fayne's car last night leads me to believe you have a good knowledge of cars," Nancy went on.

"This is true," Willy commented. "Her brother is a race-car driver."

Lionel Hornby stepped forward. "Ms. Dumont, these are very serious accusations. Do you have anything to say?"

Annelise stared sullenly down at the warm-up pants. "No, nothing. It is nonsense."

Nancy shot Annelise a long, probing look, then asked, "Would you be willing to show us what you have in your gym bag?"

Annelise looked alarmed. "My bag? No, it is personal. There is nothing in there!"

"Then why not show us?" said Cheryl.

Murmurs from Helga, Willy, Marta, and the other runners showed the general agreement to Nancy's suggestion. Annelise seemed to shrink inside her warm-up suit. Finally she turned to Nancy and muttered, "I will show you."

Annelise opened the gym bag, reached under some folded jerseys, and pulled out a bulging manila envelope.

"My film!" Eric exclaimed, grabbing for the envelope. "I was sure it had been destroyed."

A copy of *Der Läufer* was also in the bag. Taking the magazine, Nancy flipped to page twenty-three and saw that it had been neatly cut out. She pulled out the page Cheryl had received with the threatening message; it was a perfect fit.

"Ms. Dumont," Mr. Hornby said, clearing his throat. "This is proof that you threatened and harassed a fellow athlete. Such behavior is outrageous and completely unacceptable. You must understand that the referee will have to—"

"He will not," Annelise said in a tightly controlled voice. "I withdraw from the games and renounce my victory." She gave a bitter laugh. "It is the best hundred meters I have ever run. I might have won, even without . . ." Her voice trailed off.

Cheryl stepped very close in front of Annelise and looked directly into her eyes. "Why, Annelise? What did we ever do to you?"

Annelise turned her head to avoid Cheryl's gaze. "Nothing," she said. "It is . . . before I left to come here, my father became very ill. I thought this might be my last chance to show him a gold medal, and I wanted to be sure of winning. I was not in my right mind, I think."

She looked around at them but didn't seem to see any of them. "Excuse me, I must go now. I want to be by myself. When you want me, I will be in the locker room," she said. With that, she began to push through the crowd.

"But what about the hundred-meter sprint?" one of the other runners demanded. "Are we going to have to run it again, or what?"

"That's up to the referee," Mr. Hornby said. "Martin?"

The referee stroked his chin for a moment before saying, "Ordinarily, if the winner has to be disqualified, the second-place runner takes first place, the third-place runner takes second place, and so on. But from what I hear, we have a little problem with that procedure in this case."

The head finish judge stepped forward. "That's right, Martin," he said. "My judges don't agree about who took second and third places. Marta Schmidt and Cheryl Pierce were clocked in at the same instant. It doesn't happen often, but I'd have to say that we have a dead heat for second place."

As the little crowd buzzed over this new development, Mr. Hornby, the head finish-line judge, and the referee moved to one side and talked for a few moments. Then the judge turned and said in a loud voice, "It is my decision that the hundred-meter sprint was won jointly by Marta Schmidt and Cheryl Pierce. Each of them will receive the gold medal."

Cheryl let out a squeal of delight, then whirled around and gave an astonished Marta a hug. A moment later, Helga solemnly shook Cheryl's hand, then broke into a smile. Eric was practically skipping around them with his camera, trying to capture the scene from every angle.

Everyone began to applaud, but Cheryl turned to them and raised her arms for silence. In a voice that carried all the way to the grandstand, she said, "You should all know that the real champion here, the one who deserves a gold medal more than any of us, is that champion detective, Nancy Drew!"